Outlaw's Daughter

The Outlaw Series:
Book Three
By

Sherry Derr-Wille

Published by
Melange Books, LLC
White Bear Lake, MN 55110
www.melange-books.com

Outlaw's Daughter, Book The Outlaw Series: Book 3 ~

ISBN: 978-1-61235-741-6 Print

Cover Art by Lynsee Lauritsen

Outlaw's Daughter
Book Three of the Outlaw
By Sherry Derr-Wille

Jesse Tyler spent her life riding with her father's outlaw gang. When she sees her chance to escape she takes it, only to catch a bullet in her back from one of her father's men. Waking to find a lawman at her bedside she knows it's only a matter of time before she loses her life at the end of a rope.

After losing his wife and unborn child when the Tyler gang robbed the bank in the town where Russ Martin was the sheriff, Russ only wants to see a Tyler hang. Instead of the satisfaction he hoped to gain from Clay Tyler's death, Russ learns of the two youngest members of the gang Gary and Jesse Tyler. When Jesse Tyler appears in Loveland, Missouri, the town where Russ is the sheriff, he has a decision to make. Can he come to love her in the way she deserves to be loved?

I would like to dedicate this series to Kathryn Struck, the publisher who first took a change on me, an unknown author. The rest, as they say, is history.

Prologue

Slack Creek, Texas - 1885

The train arrived in Slack Creek early on Thursday evening. Before going to the Sheriff's office, Russ Martin again read the telegram he'd received just days earlier.

RUSS - WILL TYLER DEAD - CLAY TYLER WOUNDED - TRAIL IN SLACK CREEK THURSDAY - WILL TRY TO POSTPONE HANGING UNTIL YOU ARRIVE - TOM.

So few words and yet they changed his life, changed his outlook.

Four years earlier, the Tyler gang had ridden into his town, into Stillwater, Oklahoma Territory. Four years ago, a stray bullet had taken the life of his wife, Ellie. Four years ago, his own bullet had ended Ed Tyler's life. Four years ago, everything he'd ever known became meaningless.

He'd missed the trial, but hoped he wouldn't miss the hanging. More than anything else, he wanted to see Clay Tyler pay for what his family had done.

Groups of people milled in the main street. He didn't have to ask anyone about the outcome of the morning's trial. The jubilation on their faces told him Clay Tyler would surely hang the next morning.

He wasted no time in getting to Tom Claxton's office. He'd met Tom just after he and Ellie were married, just after he took the job of sheriff in Stillwater. Tom had been visiting family and stopped in to meet the new sheriff. They formed an instant friendship. Tom consoled him after Ellie's death, first with a visit and later with long letters.

"Russ, it's good to see you. Guess I don't have to ask how you're

1

feeling. It's written all over your face."

"It's good to see you, too, Tom," Russ replied. "Can I see him?"

"Of course you can, but I'd better warn you, you won't find what you expect."

"What do you mean?"

"Clay Tyler isn't much more than a boy. I'd be surprised if he's even nineteen. He ain't hardly said a word since I put him in his cell, not even at his trial. Seems like he's just trying to accept what tomorrow morning will bring."

"Nineteen?" Russ repeated. He'd heard what Tom said, but had trouble believing Clay's age. Had Ed been so young? He couldn't remember what the man even looked like.

"That's about what I reckon. He hardly has the beginnings of a beard. Such a waste, but he's a Tyler, and you know what they are."

Russ nodded. There was no use in trying to figure anything else. He wanted to see at least one of the monsters that had killed Ellie hang for their crime.

Tom got to his feet, and Russ followed him to the cell area. A lantern burned, bathing Clay in an eerie light.

"Someone here to see you, boy," Tom said.

Clay raised his head and looked into Russ' eyes. "Did you come to see the condemned man, Mister?"

"Guess you could say as much," Russ replied. "I'm Russ Martin. I won't make no bones about the fact that I came to see you hang. You killed my wife when you robbed the bank in Stillwater."

"Where?"

"Stillwater. In Oklahoma Territory. You must remember. It's the town where Ed got killed."

Clay nodded, tears beginning to spill down his cheeks. "I'm right sorry, Mister. I don't remember towns. I don't remember much, but I remember Ed gettin' killed. Do you know who done it?"

Russ swallowed hard. "I did. At least I think I did. Everyone was shooting. I like to think it was my bullet, like to think I made him pay for what you did to Ellie."

"Ellie? Was she your wife? You don't have to answer. If she wasn't your wife, you wouldn't be here, would you? They're gonna' hang me in

2

the mornin'. Would you mind if I talked to you for a while?"

Russ looked at Tom who merely shrugged his shoulders as though he didn't understand the boy's motives. "Guess it won't hurt none."

"I don't want him here." Clay pointed at Tom. "Only you."

Russ nodded and waited for Tom to leave and close the door before he pulled a chair up close to the bars of the cell.

"You must think I've lost my mind, askin' to talk to you and all," Clay began, "but I have to talk to someone. I can't talk to a preacher. It wouldn't be right, me bein' who I am and all."

Russ nodded. He could understand about the preacher. He'd not been in church since Ellie's funeral, not confessed his part in Ed's death to anyone but himself, even though everyone in town thought he'd been the one to bring the man down.

"Why me?" he finally said.

"Because you shot Ed. You know what it's like to kill a man. Most folks don't know. They just don't know what you carry around inside of you. It don't go away. I want you to know about the Tylers, all of 'em. I want you to understand we didn't start out this way. It won't help me none, but maybe it will do some good for Gary and Jesse."

"Gary and Jesse?" Russ said.

"Gary's been ridin' with us for the past three years. They always call him the masked one. Can't understand why Pa hasn't let his name be known, but he will. Gary's different from the rest of us. He don't belong with Pa."

"What do you mean he doesn't belong?"

Clay remained silent for a long moment, as if he wondered whether he was doing the right thing. Slowly the words began to come and Russ listened, trying to understand their meaning.

"He … he should have gone on to school, got an education, made something of himself. He'll never adjust to our kind of life. He can't pull the trigger, even to shoot a rabbit. He cries a lot at night, when he thinks no one's awake. I know he hates what he's become, but he can't leave. He's got a price on his head. He'll hang, just like I'll hang."

"How old is he?" Russ was intrigued with the Tyler he'd only heard referred to as 'the masked one' in the past.

"Gary's gonna turn eighteen in the fall. You'd think he would have learned to do as Pa says by now, but he hasn't. He just takes his beatings and does the same things over and over again."

Russ shook his head to rid himself of the image of an intelligent young man being forced into the life Clay described. "What about this Jesse? What's he like?"

For the first time, Clay laughed. "Jesse ain't a he, Jesse's a she. She just turned sixteen a few weeks back. Doubt she'll ever see twenty, though. If she ain't dead by then, Pa will sell her off to some bordello in Mexico, probably to someone like Isabella. Pa seems right fond of that old whore. They'll work something out. A fiery redhead with green eyes will bring a handsome price. Knowin' Pa, he'll make some sort of deal to get part of her earnings, too."

"A girl?" Russ was unable to believe his ears. "I've never heard of a girl riding with the Tylers."

"Don't reckon you have. Pa just went back to get her a few weeks back."

Russ listened, intrigued by the words. Little by little, Clay told him about Jesse. Little by little, Russ began to picture a young girl treated worse than an animal by her father and brothers.

"She's like Gary. She just don't belong," Clay finally said.

"So why tell me about the two of them?"

"I can't save either of them from Pa or my brother, Frank, for that matter. Maybe by tellin' you about them, I can save my soul, if not my life. It probably won't ever happen, but someday you may hear one of them has been caught. Could be you might remember what I told you about them. I'd like to think maybe you'd tell folks the truth about them. The thought of either of them bein' hanged makes me sick."

"Why do you think I'd ever lift a finger to help a Tyler, especially after what you've done to me?"

"I don't know. I just had a feelin' when I saw you. I know you hate us. I even know you only came here to see me hang, but you don't strike me as a man who would let kids like Gary and Jesse pay for something they ain't done. With me, it's different. I've done everything I've been accused of. I became what Pa wanted me to be, and I deserve whatever I get. I'm ready to die. At least I won't have to follow Pa's orders or face Frank's bullwhip anymore."

"I can't say I'll ever come to the rescue of a Tyler," Russ said "It goes against my grain. I will watch you hang tomorrow and then I'm going to start a new life. I plan to get away from this area, away from anyone who even knows the name of Caleb Tyler. He ruined my life once. I won't let him do it again. Maybe you can't understand it, but I doubt I'll ever attend another hanging after today. Watching you die will close this chapter of my life, and I swear I'll never so much as think about the Tylers again, as long as I live."

Clay smiled. "I can understand how you feel, but don't expect the Tylers to disappear from your life so easily. Once Caleb touches you, you ain't never the same. Because of him, you've killed a man. Now, you've come to see me hang. Believe me, you will never be the same again, and Caleb will enter your life whether you want him to or not."

* * * *

"Well, that's done," Tom said, once the trap door opened and Clay Tyler dropped to his death. "Will you be going back to Stillwater on the train or can I persuade you to stay on for a few days?"

"Neither," Russ replied. "I'm moving on. I'm going to get as far away from here as I can."

"I don't understand. Don't you want to be close enough to know when someone catches another of the Tylers?"

"One hanging in a lifetime is more than enough. I'm going to start over, forget I ever heard the name of Tyler."

"What did he say to you last night?"

"More than I wanted to hear. It doesn't matter what he said. What matters is how I heard it."

Russ turned away from Tom just in time to see the undertaker removed Clay Tyler's lifeless body from the enclosure beneath the gallows.

* * * *

The conversation with Clay rang in Russ' mind as he boarded the train. Where would this train take him? What would his life be like? Could he really start over? Could he forget what the Tylers did to Ellie, to him?

'You have to start over again, Russ' Ellie's voice sounded in his ears.

If watching Clay Tyler hang didn't bring him back, nothing could. He needed to put all of it out of his mind and find someone to love and to raise a family.

Chapter One

Clarkston, Nebraska - April, 1882

Jesse Tyler closed the worn Bible and rose from the chair. After her father's return in January, her mother began to slip away, as though she no longer cared for life.

Jesse could not remember when her father had lived at home. She had only been five or six when he first left. Now in another week she would turn thirteen and be a woman. In another year, her father would return to the farm and take her away with him like he had done with her brothers.

Over the past five years, Caleb returned to the farm once a year, taking Frank, Ed, Will, Clay, and now even Gary away with him. At first, her mother believed Caleb took the boys to work with him on a ranch in Texas. It didn't take long for stories of the Outlaw Caleb Tyler and his ruthless sons to reach Clarkston.

Just last summer, she'd heard how Ed had been killed in a small Oklahoma town. As usual, stories of Caleb's exploits brought looks of hatred from the people in town.

In January, Caleb returned to take her last remaining brother, Gary, with him. Now only Jesse and her mother were left to struggle with the farm.

Although Gary promised to keep her safe, Caleb's parting words overshadowed the promise her brother made. Two years younger than Gary, she prayed Caleb would forget she existed.

Her mother moaned softly, and Jesse returned to the parlor. "Can I get you something, Ma?"

"Just hold the basin. I no longer have the strength," her mother whispered.

Jesse held the basin while her mother vomited her breakfast, mixed with blood. When Laura lay back against the pillows, she reached out to touch Jesse's hand.

"When I'm gone, get away from here. Don't let him do this to you."

"I will, I promise, Ma," Jesse replied, wondering where she would go and how she would live.

She waited for her mother to fall asleep before going to the kitchen. After rinsing the basin with the last of the water, she took the empty pail, out to the pump to refill it.

"I hate him!" She pumped with furious energy, wishing she had the strength to drive off Caleb.

If only Caleb had stayed away, everything would be different. Gary would be in St. Louis going to school, and her mother wouldn't be dying.

Caleb had beaten Laura before. This time his anger over Gary's thirst for an education and Laura's insistence he should be allowed to pursue his dream, brought on an especially vicious attack, one from which Laura hadn't recovered.

She finished pumping the water and turned toward the house. At the end of the lane, she noticed a buggy with two people in it.

No one ever stopped out here. She dismissed the visitors without giving them much thought.

"Are you Jesse?" someone called.

Turing back, she saw the couple had pulled into the dooryard. She set down the bucket and hurried to greet them, to be hospitable.

"Depends on who's askin'," she replied. She marveled at the size of the man who got out of the carriage.

"I'm Reverend David Long and this is my wife, Hattie."

For the first time, Jesse focused on the woman. Blinking her eyes, she looked at her again. The resemblance to her mother disturbed her.

"I'm your Aunt Hattie, dear, your mother's sister," the woman said.

"I've … I've heard Ma talk about you," Jesse stammered.

The man held out his hand, and she hid her own hands, suddenly aware of the calluses and dirt, which hadn't mattered moments earlier.

"I'd shake your hand, Reverend, but I'm all dirty."

"Don't ever apologize for the dirt from honest labor, child," he said.

8

Jesse hung her head and lowered her eyes. "Where are my manners? I should have invited you in right off. Ma would skin me alive, if she had the strength. I have some coffee on the stove and some bread I made yesterday."

She turned away from the woman, still stunned by the uncanny resemblance Hattie Long had to her mother, and led them into the house. For the first time, in too many months, she looked at her home. She remembered how her mother had always prided herself on the neat appearance of her house. These past few months, there had been no time for keeping things neat and clean, no time for anything but doing chores and tending to her mother's needs.

She picked up a towel from the table and wiped out two coffee cups for the people who had followed her into the house. "I hope you don't mind takin' your coffee black. I've been savin' the cream for Ma, and I ain't had time to skim it off this morning."

"Black will be just fine, child," David said. "How long has your mother—"

A fit of coughing from behind the curtain prompted Jesse to get to her feet and hurry to her mother's side. Behind her, she heard her guests get up from their chairs and follow her, but she paid them no mind.

"Are you all right, Ma? Can I get you anything?"

Laura didn't open her eyes. "My Bible, Jesse," she whispered hoarsely. "I want my Bible."

Jesse picked up the worn book from the chair where she'd left it and handed it to her mother. "We got company, Ma. There's a preacher in town now. He came out to see you. He brought along his wife, she says she's your sister—

Before she could finish, Laura opened her eyes. "Hattie? Is Hattie here? I must see her."

"Yes, Laura, I'm here. I wish I had known how ill you are, I would have come to you sooner." The woman knelt beside the day bed.

"I got chores to do, Ma. I'll go out and do them while you and Mrs. Long have yourselves a good visit."

Jesse left the room, relieved to have someone else to care for her mother.

"Are you all right, child?" David asked, putting his hand on her shoulder.

Jesse nodded. "You'll have to excuse me, Reverend. Like I told Ma, I've got chores to do."

"Let me help you."

"I can do for myself. Ma ain't got long. I've known it for weeks. I'd like it if you'd read to her from the Bible. The Twenty-third Psalm is her favorite. I read other passages to her, but she always insists I read the Psalm to her first. She likes to say the words along with me, so when you read it, don't go too fast. I'll be back in as soon as I finish what I have to do outside."

Jesse left the house and went out to the barn. She'd milked the cow this morning, but there were eggs to gather and chickens to feed. She wondered how long she would be able to keep the chickens.

The money her father left in January had dwindled quickly. She'd tried to be careful with it, not to spend more than she had, but it seemed as though the price of coffee, sugar, and flour rose every time she went into town. She often thought Mr. Clark raised the prices because of his hatred of the Tylers, but she tried not to dwell on such dark thoughts. Mr. Clark had founded Clarkston and, like the teacher said, he'd done a lot for the community. He'd started a church and even acted as the preacher for the services held in the tavern.

Thinking of the church in town, she remembered when it first started. Her Ma had been so anxious to go, she had told them that come Sunday she would scrub them all until their skin burned and get them dressed in their best clothes so that they could walk the five miles into town. Of course, it never happened. Ma had gone to town in the middle of the week, only to be told that the church was for the good people of Clarkston, not the Tylers.

Even the rejection of the good citizens of Clarkston hadn't extinguished the fire of Laura Tyler's faith. She insisted they read from the Bible every night and even prayed for the salvation of the townspeople, the people who wanted nothing to do with the Tyler family.

As soon as she finished her chores, Jesse returned to the house. There would be things she'd need to do, especially with company. She knew her mother would be upset if she didn't prepare a meal, no matter how meager, for their guests.

When she entered the house, the expression on Mrs. Long's face told her Laura Tyler had passed on to a better life. There would be no more long hours spent listening to her mother cough. No more nights sleeping in a chair to be close by in case her mother needed her. No more reading from the Bible to ease her mother's mind.

"I'm sorry, Jesse. She slipped away while I held her hand," Hattie said, tears spilling from her eyes.

"It's best," Jesse replied, too hardened from the last few months to cry. "She's been powerful sick. I knew she wanted to go home to the Lord. I'd best fix us somethin' to eat. When we finish, I'll get her ready for burial. She wants to rest out back of the house with Andy."

"Andy?" David said.

"My brother. He died right after he was born. Ma said he couldn't get his breath, and he died. They buried him out back of the house. She wants to rest close to him."

David nodded. "I'll go out to the barn and see if I can find some wood for a coffin. Once it's ready, I'll dig the grave."

With Hattie's help, Jesse washed her mother's body and dressed her in the one good dress she owned. She debated about putting the wedding ring back on her mother's finger, but decided against it. Laura took the ring off in January and never put it back on. She'd broken the hold Caleb held over her, and Jesse refused to tie her to someone she so despised, even in death.

With the burial finished, Hattie helped Jesse to pack her meager possessions. As the carriage pulled from the dooryard, Jesse said good-bye to the only life she had ever known, and went into town to live with the strangers who professed to be her family.

Chapter Two

March, 1885

Jesse finished cleaning the parsonage and set about preparing supper. With her aunt at the church for a Ladies Aid meeting and her uncle visiting a sick parishioner, she would be responsible for the evening meal. She didn't mind. Unlike the life she had lived three years earlier, her household tasks had become a labor of love.

Since her mother's death, she had grown from a frightened child to a woman. She smiled as she thought about Walter Carson. He would be coming over after supper to ask Uncle David for her hand. Walter had been working the farm ever since she moved into town. Under his expert hand, he managed to produce a good crop every year.

Ever since Advent, he'd been coming around the parsonage. At first, he came to talk about the farm and to tell her how well the fields were producing, but soon the talk turned to the future. Since she would soon be sixteen, he had asked if she would mind if he asked Uncle David for her hand. Of course, she hadn't objected. She fancied herself in love with the tall lanky farmer and knew she could be happy with him.

A knock at the door turned her mind from Walter and the life they would soon share to her unknown visitor. She dried her hands on the towel she kept beside her while she worked and hurried to answer the insistent knocking.

As she opened the door, she froze. Caleb stood in the doorway, smiling at her, the way he always smiled at her. "It's time, Jesse Girl, time for you to come with me. Your brothers are powerful excited to see

12

you again."

"Stay away from me, Pa. Just stay away from me. I have a life here. You can't make me go with you."

"I can make you do anything I want you to do," Caleb growled, grasping her arm before she could run from him. "Now, you're comin' with me."

Jesse tried to strike out, to free herself from his vise-like grip, but her struggles only infuriated her father. "If you won't come like your brothers, you'll come with me my way."

Before she could protest, Caleb drew back his fist. The instant pain of the blow sent her into the bliss of unconsciousness.

* * * *

Jesse fought her way back from the black depths. Her jaw hurt and her body ached. She tried to stretch, but ropes bound her hands and feet making it impossible for her to move.

"She's startin' to come around, Caleb. I didn't think she'd ever come to," Jesse heard a strange woman say. "You shouldn't have hit her so hard. You could have killed her. She ain't one of your boys, you know. She's a delicate little thing. Let me untie her and get her something to eat."

"Leave her be, Lottie. You can feed her, but you can't untie her. I know what's best. She's got more spunk than the boys. She'd try to run away, and I can't have her goin' back to that preacher."

Jesse opened her eyes and saw a large woman bending over her. The woman reached out her hand and stroked Jesse's hair.

"You poor little thing," the woman crooned. "Drink some of this broth."

"I don't want anything from you," Jesse whispered.

Without warning, Caleb pulled her hair and forced her to look into his face. "You'll do as Lottie says. If it were up to me, I wouldn't feed you 'til you begged for it."

"Then why did you take me away? I had a good life. I—"

Caleb slapped her hard, bringing tears to her eyes. Before he could again strike her, the woman intervened.

"You've hurt her enough, Caleb. You go in the other room while I tend to her needs. When I'm finished, I'll take care of you."

"Who are you?" Jesse said, after Caleb left.

"It don't matter, child. Your Pa, he's got a mean streak. I don't think he'd give killin' you a second thought. He told me he couldn't tolerate you bein' brought up by no preacher. You're the only one who can take care of yourself now. Do as he says and he won't hurt you as much. Now drink this broth. I have to get in and take care of his needs. You'll be ridin' out in the mornin', and you can't do it on an empty stomach."

Jesse sipped the rich broth and then closed her eyes. Her worst nightmare had come true. Caleb had come for her and changed her life forever. She fell asleep almost instantly, dreaming of what could have been, of what would never be.

* * * *

Jesse lost track of the days and nights they spent on the trail to Mexico. When they hadn't been able to find a place to stay, they were forced to spend the night in the open. Even then, she hadn't been free. Caleb would bind her hand and foot. Once she was securely bound, he would attach a rope around her neck, tying the other end to his own wrist. She knew she had no means of escape, no chance for a better life.

"Over the next rise is your new home, Jesse Girl," Caleb said, late one afternoon. "You'll see your brothers tonight and tomorrow you'll start working for Mendoza. He said he could use a girl at the house. Just remember, even though he'll treat you good, if I hear one word about you tryin' to leave, I swear I'll whip the hide off your body."

Jesse merely nodded. She had said very little during the trip south. There was nothing to say. In the past weeks, her father stripped every shred of normalcy from her life, leaving her frightened and withdrawn.

A crude shack came into view and Jesse immediately recognized Gary tending the fire. Caleb reined his horse to a halt and swung out of the saddle. Jesse merely waited for him to yank her from the back of the horse, the way he'd done so many times before.

Once on the ground, each of her brothers embraced her. She hardly recognized any of them. They had become men while riding with Caleb with hardened features. Only Gary treated her tenderly, untying her wrists and holding her tightly.

14

"I'm sorry," he whispered. "I tried to keep him from comin' for you, I honestly did. Come over to the fire, and I'll get you something to eat."

"I don't want anything from you," she spat, unable to control her emotions.

"Look, neither of us can change anything. Just do as Pa says, and you'll be fine."

"Come over here, Jesse Girl," Caleb shouted, interrupting Gary. "I've got somethin' for you."

Jesse followed Gary toward the fire, afraid not to obey, afraid of taking another beating.

"This is for you," Caleb said, holding out a hand-tooled holster, which cradled a pearl handled colt revolver. "You're goin' to learn how to use it. Clay will show you how to shoot. Gary will teach you about the horses. By the end of the summer, I expect you to shoot as well as Clay, ride as well as Gary, and be as ruthless as Frank. Do I make myself clear?"

Jesse nodded. None of this made any sense to her. Why did God let Caleb take her away with him? What had she ever done to deserve such a severe punishment?

"Do as he says," Gary whispered to her, as they cleaned up from supper. "It ain't worth the pain."

"Are you as good a shot as Clay? As ruthless as Frank?" she demanded.

Gary hung his head. "No, I ain't, and I suffer for it. I can't shoot to kill, and I can't hit the target. Believe me, both Pa and Frank enjoy watching me fail. It gives them an excuse to beat me. If it wasn't for the way I handle horses, they would have killed me long ago. Listen to me, do as they say and you won't get hurt. Don't be like me."

Gary went on about his business, giving Jesse time to think, time to digest what he had just told her.

When bedtime finally came, Caleb again secured her hands and feet. Bitter tears stung her eyes as he tied the rope around her neck.

"Why bother, Pa? There's no place for me to go. I don't think I could ever find my way back. Why don't you just let me sleep peacefully?"

Caleb said nothing, nor did he remove the ropes. Alone and scared, she cried herself to sleep, afraid of what the morning might bring.

* * * *

Jesse had worked in the Mendoza household for almost three weeks. To her surprise, almost everyone in the household spoke flawless English. Although she worked hard, she didn't mind the tasks they asked her to do.

She'd just finished washing the floor of the dining room, when the Mendoza's five-year-old daughter, Carmalita, came into the room crying. Touched by the child's tears, she knelt down to comfort her.

"Are you hurt?" she said to the child.

Carmalita shook her head. "I…I tore my new dress."

Jesse examined the three-corner tear near the hem of the child's garment. "I have to wait for this floor to dry. I saw a room upstairs for sewing. Come with me, and I'll mend it for you."

In the sewing room, the child stared at her, wide-eyed, as she made fine stitches to repair the tear. When she finished, she could hardly even see where the fabric had been torn.

"There, this will be our little secret. No one will ever know what happened."

The little girl hugged Jesse tightly before running off to play. Jesse carefully put away the needle and thread. Once everything was returned to its place, she closed the door silently. She knew she shouldn't have come up to this room, but Carmalita's grateful hug made her glad she acted on impulse.

When she came downstairs, the woman who told her what to do pulled her aside. "You must have done something very bad," the woman cautioned. "Senor and Senora Mendoza want to see you in the library. If you value your life, you will act very humble and beg their forgiveness for whatever it is you have done."

Cautiously, Jesse entered the library.

"Come here," Senor Mendoza ordered.

Jesse did as he told her, keeping her eyes downcast as she went to his side.

"Are you afraid of me?" He lifted her chin so he could look into her eyes.

"What have I done?" she said.

"Sit down," Senora Mendoza advised. "Carmalita told us she tore her dress when she was playing, and you mended it for her."

Jesse began to panic. How could she have expected such a small child not to tell her mother what had happened? "I'm sorry. She seemed so sad I only wanted to make her happy. I know I shouldn't have touched the things in the sewing room, but I put everything back where I found it."

"Did you think we would punish you for helping our daughter?" Senora Mendoza pressed. "On the contrary, we are very happy you helped her. I've never seen finer stitching. I know you will be going north soon, but when you return, I would like to have you do all of my sewing. The woman who has been doing it for me is getting too old to see her work. It is time she rested."

Jesse couldn't believe her ears. Soon she would no longer have to scrub the floors and keep the house clean. She would be able to spend her days doing something she enjoyed.

Later that afternoon, when she left the house, Clay met her at the door. "I didn't expect to see you," she greeted him. "What happened to Pa? He's always here waiting for me."

"Pa and Will rode north to check out a town not too far from the border. It will be our first job. You'll see, Jes, once you start ricin' with us, you'll come to enjoy it."

Jesse turned to face her older brother. She couldn't understand how he could believe the words he just spoke. "Does Gary enjoy it?" she snapped.

"No, but learn from his mistakes, Jes. Do as you're told and things will be much easier for you."

"Don't you understand, if I do the things you and the others do, I'll surely go to Hell. I can't rob banks and murder innocent people and still be a Christian."

Clay grabbed her arm tightly and turned her until her face almost touched his. "Don't be a fool, Jes. You'll learn it, just like the rest of us. There ain't no God for the Tylers. If you insist on hangin' onto the hogwash Ma and that preacher told you, keep it to yourself. If Pa and Frank hear you, they'll beat you bloody."

Jesse withdrew into her own private shell and tried to block out the words Clay had spoken. She'd loved him once. He was her older brother and someone to whom she looked. Now, he'd become as heartless as her father.

Chapter Three

Missouri, 1887

Jesse woke and shivered in her bedroll. The Eastern sky above the hills had already begun to lighten with streaks of pink and blue, showing the promise of predawn.

Just once, just once she would like to wake up in a soft bed and be warm.

Last night's campfire had burned down to a few glowing coals. Still exhausted, she forced herself to rise and feed the fire to begin preparing breakfast.

As she worked, she marveled at the beauty of the canyon. They'd been camped here, alongside a herd of mustangs, for the last three weeks, and she realized just how much she enjoyed the solitude. The crispness of the morning told her winter would soon arrive. One more job and they would be going to Mexico.

Her preparations were made silently to avoid waking the sleeping men. Their contented snores assured her she'd been successful.

Behind her, slept her father and oldest brother, Frank. They were her cruel captors, her jailers. She'd become little more than their slave, their property. Next to them, slept her brother, Gary. Dear Gary, less than two years separated them and yet he seemed to be much older. For the past two years, he'd been her protector, her buffer. How many beatings had he taken for her? How many times had she washed the cuts on his back from Frank's bullwhip?

On the other side of the fire was Ruben Walden. He and Jeb Morris joined them after Will and Clay were killed. Both Ruben and Jeb were certain she would belong to them once they arrived in Mexico. Last night, with Jeb in some town sizing up the bank, Ruben had begun pawing her. Knowing the inevitability of it, yet sickened by the idea, she fought back, raking his face with her fingernails. He slapped her and sent her reeling backwards almost into the fire.

Never, she silently vowed, never would he touch her again. Never would she allow a man to paw her like some wild animal. As usual, Gary came to her rescue.

She put thoughts of the present aside and searched her memory of the past. Why had it started? Why had it continued? She'd been so safe with her Aunt Hattie and Uncle David. She'd lived with them for almost three years after her mother died. She'd even begun to believe her father would not come for her as he came for each of her brothers before her. Then suddenly, out of nowhere, he appeared and took her away from the security of the only real home, the only real love, she'd ever known.

Two years had passed since her Pa and Frank took her with them on a job. Two years since Will and Clay had been killed in Slack Creek. Two years since she'd experienced any sense of freedom. Two years since she'd become her father's prisoner.

The night before Slack Creek, Gary and Frank argued until the early hours of morning. "Good grief, Frank, she's only a baby. We don't need her," she could still hear Gary say.

"She's almost sixteen years old. You were fourteen the first time. We all were. She's a Tyler. It seems to me the time has come for her to learn what being one of us means."

Early the next morning, they'd ridden out. Caleb, Frank, Will, Clay, Gary, and Jesse, the surviving members of the Tyler family.

They rode into a small town, hardly more than a few buildings strung together over the open prairie. Almost in the center, she located the bank, a small wooden building that looked no different from any of the other buildings along the dusty main street.

Calmly, Pa, Will, and Clay entered the bank, followed by Frank, Gary, and her last.

She remembered the relief of wearing men's clothing, knowing her hat hid her hair in the same manner her bandanna hid her face. The shame of entering a bank with gun in hand still remained unbearable.

The weight of the gun on her hip and the feel of it in her hand were alien to her. 'Thou shalt not steal,' echoed in her mind, as she walked slowly, flanked by Gary and Frank.

She moved as though in a trance until three shots rang out, bringing reality. Before her eyes, Will and Clay fell to the floor, bleeding.

"Will! Clay!" she screamed, trying to get closer to them.

"Keep that fool quiet," her father barked.

Frank's hand encircled her arm like a steel band, and he dragged her out of the bank. He acted like he couldn't hear her screams. Once outside the building, he literally threw her onto her horse and gave it a whack on the rump.

"We can't leave them," she protested, but no one listened. All around her, gunfire exploded as the four of them rode out of town.

They rode for what seemed like hours until, at last, Caleb assured them they were no longer being followed and turned his horse back in the direction of their camp. To her surprise, both Gary and Caleb had been wounded, although neither acknowledged their wounds during the ride. The skill, with which Frank removed the bullets, amazed Jesse.

All the time Frank attended to her father and brother, Jesse cried. She cried from fear, for the loss of her brothers, as well as for Gary and her father. Both were pale from the amount of blood they had lost.

Once Frank finished, he turned on her. "Shut up, you little fool!" he shouted. "I hope you watched me just now. Don't kid yourself. You'll have to do this more than once."

"No," Jesse managed to sniff. "I can't and I won't."

"You will and you can," Frank said, as he calmly walked toward his horse and untied his bullwhip from the saddle horn.

"Will Pa and Gary die?" she said, unable to take her eyes from Frank's whip.

"They won't die," Frank spat. "Ain't it enough you killed Will and Clay today? Haven't you had enough blood?"

"I didn't kill them. I didn't," she screamed.

"Of course you did, because of you they were careless."

"You don't even know if they're dead. You just left them there."

"They're dead. If not by those bullets, they'll hang. Do you understand what it means to be a Tyler, Jes? Someday we'll all die by the gun or the rope. You won't get a choice. We've killed more men, women, and even children than we can count. No matter what the number, you can bet every lawman around has doubled and even tripled the number by now."

Jesse shook with fear, not at Frank's words, but at the crack of his whip as it came so close to her cheek. She could feel the breeze it generated.

"A penny for your thoughts, Little One," Gary whispered in her ear, bringing her back to the morning's chill, to the canyon's beauty, to reality.

"Ain't worth a penny," she whispered back, wiping tears from her eyes with the back of her hand. "Let's leave here, Gary. Let's go somewhere and start over. I hear Oregon is good or California. We could change our names, we could—"

"We could get ourselves hanged before the first week was out," Gary said, not allowing her to finish. "We're wanted, Jes. Don't you remember what Pa told us? We can never hope for any life other than this one."

"Maybe you're right, but I don't want this life. I'd rather die in the first town I come to, than continue to live like this. Hanging would be a picnic compared to being Ruben's woman."

"Look, Jes, if you're going, go now, before we pull this job."

"Why?"

"Don't ask questions. Just do as I say."

Hearing the men behind her beginning to stir, she got to her feet, leaving Gary behind. She could feel him watching her as she began preparing breakfast for the men. Even with his eyes boring a hole into her back, she wondered what he'd meant.

She longed to take comfort in her mother's Bible, but it had been left at the parsonage. Silently, she repeated the words of the Twenty-third Psalm and took comfort in them. No matter what her father told her, she knew God cared for her. She only wished she could convince Gary of God's love.

Night fell and one by one, the men drifted off to sleep. Listening to them snore, she slipped out of camp, away from her father and brothers, away from the life she'd been forced to lead for the past two years.

Quietly, she led her horse away from the canyon. Once safely out of earshot, she mounted the gray mare and rode. For the first time she was as free as the wind. Above her, the sky looked like a canopy of black velvet strewn with precious gems. Beneath her, the horse flew toward the unknown, the light of the full moon illuminating the landscape.

Silvery moonlight bathed the world in an eerie glow. She wanted to sing. At last, she would be free.

The burning pain in her back came at the same instant she heard the rifle shot. Her last conscious thought centered on the pain and the realization she would never again see her beloved Aunt Hattie and Uncle David. Falling into the sweet darkness of total unconsciousness, she tumbled from the back of the horse onto the ground.

Chapter Four

Russ Martin knew he'd found the perfect town. The small farming community of Loveland, Missouri seemed as different from Stillwater as day from night. No boisterous cowboys invaded the town on Saturday nights, shooting their guns into the air. Although the people had heard of the Tyler gang, they didn't live in fear of them. Loveland sat too far north and east to be in Caleb Tyler's territory.

He ran a comb through his hair and took one last look in the mirror, preparing to walk across the street to get some breakfast. Then Brian McPhearson entered the office.

"You have to get out to the farm," Brian said, his words tumbling over themselves. "We found a girl, shot in the back."

"Slow down, Brian," Russ advised. "Take a minute to catch your breath and then tell me what's happened."

The young man took several deep breaths before continuing. "We were on our way to church," he finally managed to say. "We found a girl, lying beside the road. She'd been shot in the back."

"Girl?" Russ said. "How old is this girl?"

"Eighteen, nineteen, maybe."

"Did you know her?"

"I never laid eyes on her before."

"Can you tell me what she looks like? What she wore?"

"She's pretty. Her face is all bruised up though, and she had long red hair. She was wearing men's clothes."

"You go and get Doc Page," Russ ordered. "I'll head out to your place."

He didn't wait to see if Brian did as he'd told him to do. He knew he needed to get out to the McPhearson place and find out if his worst nightmare had come true.

Brian's description of the girl fit the one he'd heard from Clay Tyler in the Slack Creek jail. At the time, he'd prayed he could put Caleb Tyler and everything he represented behind him. Now he wondered if Clay's prediction had come true.

As he rode into the dooryard of the McPhearson farm, a large collie dog greeted him with friendly barks. The dog waited for Russ to give him a pat on the head before leaving him alone.

Tied to the porch railing, Russ spotted a gray mare, the horse Brian said had been standing next to the girl.

He dismounted and took the steps of the porch two at a time before knocking at the door.

"Come on in, Russ," John greeted him, when he opened the door. "Are Brian and Doc Page with you?"

"No, I came on ahead. Do you have any idea who she is?"

"I don't have a clue."

"What are you talking about, Pa?"

Russ turned to see Brian's twin brother, Quaid enter the room. As usual, the boy looked like he was nursing the granddaddy of a hangover. Just last night he'd seen Quaid in the tavern. Although it had been early, he had already been on his way to being drunk. It wasn't anything unusual. Over the past few months, Quaid had become a Saturday night drunk. Everyone in town had an opinion about his drinking and what it was doing to John and Brenna McPhearson.

"This is what we found on her horse," John said, handing Russ the saddlebags and guns, while ignoring his son's question.

The ornately carved pearl handled colt, with its raised 'T' made Russ sick to his stomach. He'd seen its mate two years earlier in Slack Creek and before that in Stillwater. It could only belong to one woman.

"Jesse Tyler," he said, almost unaware he'd spoken out loud

Quaid took the gun from Russ' hands. "The Tylers? Do we have one of the Tyler gang here? Which one? Why here?"

Russ listened while John told his son about finding the girl and sending Brian to town.

"The girl is Jesse Tyler," Russ added. "She may ride with the gang, but there's never been a wanted poster out on her."

"How do you know so much about the Tyler gang?" Quaid said.

"It happens to be my job to know about them," Russ replied. He didn't say the Tylers had become his obsession, nor did he tell them he knew more about the Tylers than any other lawman. He and he alone, knew about the girl named Jesse Tyler. The beautiful girl with long red hair, whose destiny had been to be a whore in a Mexican bordello or to be killed. In a matter of minutes, he would finally see her for himself.

Clay's parting words echoed in his mind. "Don't expect the Tylers to disappear from your life so easily. Once Caleb touches you, you're never the same."

"Where is she?"

"Brenna's with her in the bedroom off the parlor," John replied.

When Russ entered the downstairs bedroom, he stopped short. Jesse Tyler looked every bit as beautiful as Clay and Brian told him. As he stood, looking at the girl who lay in bed, he found neither the bruises on her face, nor the calluses on her hands could distract from her beauty. He'd found her. He'd actually found the one member of the Tyler gang no one else knew existed. Perhaps now he could let go of his hatred and begin a new life. He hadn't been able to do so when he found Clay. He hoped it would happen now that he'd found Jesse.

To Russ' surprise, she opened her eyes and stared at him in shock. Fear showed in her emerald green eyes and what little color she did have in her face drained.

"Are you Jesse, Jesse Tyler?" he said. "Can you hear me?"

Jesse ran her delicate tongue over her dry lips. "Where am I?"

"Don't worry, you're safe," he assured her.

Her eyes rested on his badge, and her voice echoed the despair in her heart. "I ... I doubt it," she whispered before closing her eyes, apparently giving in to her physical pain.

Russ wanted to hate her, yet he also wanted to comfort her, to reassure her. Before he could find the right words, Dr. Page and Brian entered the room

"So, this is my patient," Dr. Page said, lifting her wrist. "Do you know who she is yet, Russ?"

Before he could answer, Jesse again opened her eyes. "My name is

Jesse Tyler," she said, her voice little more than a whisper. "I ain't nobody's patient."

"Dr. Page ignored her protests and began his examination. Jesse winced in pain whenever he touched her. "I can't tell how deep the bullet is," he said.

* * * *

Bullet? Jesse hadn't contemplated why she rested in a soft bed or how she'd gotten there. She only knew the first person she saw had been a lawman.

She forced herself to recall the events of the past few hours. She'd left the camp, left her father and brothers and then ... then she'd been shot. Who shot her, the law, and her father, Frank, Ruben? None of them had been aware of her plans.

Could it have been Gary? No, not Gary. He'd been her protector for too long. He didn't have the stomach for killing.

"I want you to drink this, Jesse," Dr. Page said, holding out a beaker of medication to her. "It will help with the pain."

"I'm a Tyler. I don't need no help with the pain," Jesse said, through clinched teeth.

"I don't care if you think you're the President of the United States, you are going to drink this."

As much as she hated to admit it, any relief from the pain would be welcome. This pain, this terrible pain, went beyond any she'd suffered from Frank's beatings. Her resolve weakened as Dr. Page helped her drink the sweet tasting liquid. Although she fought the urge to give into the drug, she slowly slipped into a blissful, painless sleep.

* * * *

Even in the girl's weakened state, the drug took a long time to work. When she became completely oblivious to the events around her, Dr. Page turned to Brenna.

"I know you mean well, but what has to be done here won't be pretty. I suggest you get some clean towels and some hot water. Perhaps John can come in and assist us with this."

Although Russ knew Brenna wanted to stay, at the same time an excuse to leave seemed to come as a welcome suggestion. He knew she'd seen the damage the bullet did and realized she could never withstand the horrors of the operation to remove it.

"Is she really one of the Tylers, Ma?" Quaid said when she entered the parlor. "Did Russ say how much the reward will be?"

"She's definitely one of the Tylers," Russ replied, as he followed Brenna into the room. "It seems to me I told you before there was no reward for her."

"You're wrong. If she's a Tyler, there has to be a reward. There's posters out on all of that bunch, the whole lot of them."

"I meant just what I said, Quaid," Russ retorted. "There is no reward. I told you when I first got here there were no posters out on Jesse Tyler. We're the only people, outside of the Tyler gang, who even knows she exists."

Russ turned his attention away from the greedy young man. "Doc needs your help, John." With Dr. Page's message relayed, Russ returned to the downstairs bedroom and the ravages of what the bullet had done to Jesse Tyler.

* * * *

"Will she live?" Russ said anxiously, breaking the silence in which Dr. Page had worked for the past two hours.

"Yes, Russ, she'll live. Her rib stopped the bullet. Her recuperation will be a long one, but she's young. She'll sleep for at least another hour. Perhaps you can take that time to tell us about Jesse Tyler. It seems you know more about her than you've let on."

Russ nodded. Once they were seated at Brenna's kitchen table eating dinner, he related the events of the past six years. He ended the story with a final statement. "Until this morning, I'd decided Jesse Tyler didn't exist. I'd convinced myself she'd either been sold in Mexico or died, as Clay predicted."

With the story completed, he excused himself to return to the downstairs bedroom. He wanted to relieve Brian who had stayed by her bedside. For some reason, he couldn't put his finger on, he wanted to be there when she regained consciousness.

* * * *

Jesse woke in the milky period between full awareness and sleep.

She lay in a soft bed and, for the first time in weeks, she wasn't shivering from the cold. As she luxuriated in the comfort, reality sunk in. She'd been free for so short a time before someone tried to kill her and now, even if she survived, she'd traded one prison for another.

"Someday we'll all die by the gun or by the rope," she could hear Frank say. "You won't get a choice, Jes. It's what being a Tyler means."

"Jesse," someone said. "Are you awake?"

"Yes," she replied weakly, "but it don't matter none. Is a hangin' so important to you? You should have let me die."

"There will be no hanging, Jesse," the lawman said, as he entered the room. "You have my word on it."

"The word of a lawman?" She looked up at him. "I am who I am, just as you are who you are. I'm a Tyler. You should have let me die by the gun, since I ain't too fond of the rope."

The man pulled a chair closer to her bed and then took her hand. To her surprise, it wasn't the callused hand of one of her brothers, but soft and warm.

"Two years ago I met your brother, Clay—"

"Sure you did. What do you take me for, a fool? Clay is dead. He died in Slack Creek. He died because … because of me." Unbidden tears ran down her cheeks, and she closed her eyes to stop them.

"Your brother Clay died in Slack Creek, but not from his wounds. They hanged him."

The word hanged echoed through her mind. The vision of Clay dangling at the end of a rope tore at her soul. She pulled her hand free, but forced herself to listen as the man continued.

"I arrived before the hanging. Clay told me about you and Gary. Since then, I've kept up on the Tylers. There's never been a poster on you."

Jesse wondered if this man told her the truth. Why would Clay have told a lawman about her? She decided to test him further, even though her strength was nearly gone.

"What about Gary?" she demanded.

She watched, as the man debated for a long moment. "There have been posters out on him ever since Slack Creek. Clay asked me to help you and Gary, if I ever got the chance."

"Why? You're a lawman. Why would Clay want you to help us?"

"Because he said you didn't belong with your father." The man paused as though allowing the words to sink in, letting her digest what he'd just told her.

Confusion over took her and she closed her eyes. Could it be true? Was she really free? Would Gary ever know freedom?

* * * *

Russ watched Jesse. Would she believe him? Could he ever convince her she didn't have a price on her head? Could he make her trust him enough to tell him what he needed to know to catch the men who killed his wife?

"Who shot you?" He finally said, after giving her a moment to digest what he told her.

"I don't know."

"Think, Jesse. Who knew you were running away?" He knew his questions pushed her strength to the limit, but he had to know the answer.

"Only Gary, but it couldn't have been him. He's not a good shot. He doesn't have the stomach for killing. I'm positive no one followed me. It must have been Jeb."

"Jeb Morris?"

Jesse nodded. He could tell sleep was now threatening to overcome her.

"He's been checking out your bank for the last three days."

"You must be wrong. He couldn't have been in our town. I would have known him."

Jesse smiled and almost laughed. "Are you sure? I doubt it. Think back, didn't you see an old hermit, or perhaps a preacher man, or maybe just a drifter? Someone with an unkempt beard, someone who seemed to belong, and yet seemed foreign?"

Russ nodded. In his mind, he could see the preacher who'd been spouting scriptures in the tavern, damming all the patrons to the eternal fires of Hell. Then, of course, there had been the drifter, the cowboy who seemed out of place in the sleepy farming community. Could one of them have been Jeb Morris? Would Caleb and his men hit Loveland next?

"Where are they camped?" Russ probed, now desperate for an answer, any answer.

"We were camped in a box canyon about an hour's ride from where they shot me, but they ain't there now. Likely most of the way to Mexico by this time."

Russ wanted to ask more questions, wanted more answers, but he knew Jesse's strength had reached its limits. He could hear her speech growing slurred, and her eyes had closed.

He watched her drift off to sleep and marveled at how beautiful and vulnerable she appeared. He'd built her up in his mind as someone pure and untouched, but how could she be either after riding with Caleb for three years?

He was a fool. He shouldn't let her get to him. He needed a cool head. Somehow, he had to find Caleb and the others, even if he had to use her to do it.

Chapter Five

Each time Jesse awoke, she felt more rested, more alert. Her original fears had been replaced by the alien feeling of trust. Brenna and John were kind and loving people who treated her as an honored guest.

Undeserving. She was so undeserving of their kindness. How would she ever repay them?

Brenna reminded her of Aunt Hattie. She knew that kind, gentle, and loving were the only words to describe her. Jesse could feel a bond growing and enjoyed the time she spent alone with the woman.

Russ knew more about the Tylers than they knew about themselves, and this realization made her uneasy. He told her he'd seen Ed killed and talked to Clay before he was hanged. Somehow, he knew what it meant to be a Tyler.

Quaid bothered her. Although he looked like the mirror image of his brother, Brian, the similarities ended there. Where Brian's words were softly spoken, Quaid's manner was boisterous. Where Brian showed compassion toward her, Quaid's only interest seemed to be in the life she led with Caleb. Where Brian could make her smile and even laugh, Quaid made her want to lash out at him.

Little by little, she told her story. Bit by bit, those who heard her words became engrossed by what she had to say. With each telling, the words came easier, each word lifted the burden just a little bit more and set her free.

Jesse prayed each person in the room would sense her fear and her hurt as she told the story. When she felt their compassion, she started coming to grips with her past. With the uprooting of each buried memory, Jesse wept openly, while Brenna wiped the tears from her face.

"Would you like us to contact your aunt and uncle?" Brenna said, after Jesse finally told her story to its completion.

Brenna's words distressed her. More than anything else, she wanted to see Hattie and David. To her dismay, she realized she had no right to expect to resurrect her life in the parsonage. Caleb had found her there once. She couldn't be certain he wouldn't find her there again. She loved Hattie and David far too much to allow Caleb or Frank to cause them pain.

"It's best they continue to think I'm dead," she said, in a low voice. "As soon as I'm able to ride, I'll be leavin' here to start a new life. Somehow I'll repay you for your kindness, but I can't continue to endanger the people who mean the most to me."

"I'm certain you'll change your mind," John assured her. "You're tired and discouraged now. Get some sleep and think on what we've been talkin' about."

"I agree with John," Russ said, taking her hand in his. "You need your rest. Things will look different in the morning."

One by one, they all left the room. Jesse tried to make her mind quit spinning so she could go to sleep. She found Russ' actions confusing. When he talked about the Tyler gang, it seemed as though he knew them all personally and despised them as much as she did. When he talked to and about her, his voice softened. She wondered if he cared or if she only wanted someone, anyone, to care.

When sleep finally overtook her, she found it to be anything but the peaceful rest she so desperately needed.

"You're a Tyler, Jesse Girl," her father said, as he loomed in her dream. "You'll never be free. You're as good as dead."

Clay's face replaced Caleb's. "Don't believe him, Jes. You've found Russ Martin. Listen to him. He took the time to hear what I had to say. God must have thought what I told him about you and Gary wiped out what Pa made me do, 'cause I'm with Ma."

The dream faded, and Jesse longed to see Clay again. "Clay, Clay," she screamed.

She woke to someone shaking her and calling her name. Reluctantly, she forced the sleep from her body and found herself looking into Brian's blue eyes.

"Jesse," Brian said. "Wake up. You were having a nightmare."

She didn't argue. She found it a relief to see Brian and not her father standing over her. She saw no point in telling him the end of her dream had not been a nightmare, but merely an impossible dream.

* * * *

Days passed and, to Jesse's dismay, she remained in bed. "I'll never get out of this bed, will I, Doc?" she said Dr. Page at the end of the week.

"Of course you will, Jesse, but for now, you need to get your rest. You were badly wounded. You lost a lot of blood. The healing won't come quickly."

As much as she wanted to believe Dr. Page, she didn't. Although Russ kept assuring her she would be free, she fell deeper and deeper into a state of depression. What good would it do to be free if she lost the use of her legs? The prison of being a cripple would be far worse than any imprisonment with her father.

"Why God," she continued to pray daily. "Why are you punishing me? Hasn't Caleb hurt me enough?"

Only in her dreams did she find freedom. It was at those times when she heard the answer to her prayers. "*Trust in Me, Jesse. Believe me when I say I know what I'm doing. I have plans for you, but the suffering must last a bit longer.*"

Chapter Six

Russ sat in his office reviewing the events of the past week. In his wildest dreams, he had never expected to find any of the Tylers, especially not Jesse.

He recalled his conversation with Clay and thought of the words the young man had used. 'Once Caleb Tyler crosses your path, you won't ever be free of him. You'll never be able to run far enough away to escape him. None of us can. The only escape we can hope for is death. In my case, I'll be free before another day passes. In Jesse's case, I'm afraid she'll never be free.'

Could Clay have been right? Would he never be free of Caleb Tyler? Would Jesse have to live in fear of the man for the rest of her days?

His thoughts of Jesse confused him. He wanted to hate her, wanted her to be more like Caleb and Frank so he could dismiss her easily from his mind. Unfortunately, he felt none of the emotions he wanted to feel. She haunted him.

How could he even feel compassion toward her? Had she become important in his life? He couldn't let that happen. He couldn't let her have even a small part of his affections. If it hadn't been for Caleb, Ellie and he would have had a house full of kids by now. They'd have been happy. Jesse must never become more than bait for an elaborate trap to catch as many of the Tylers as he could.

His mind continued to spin with his thoughts of Jesse. He remembered the conversation they engaged in earlier in the week. She had asked him if he believed in God. His negative answer seemed to have saddened her. He wondered if she truly believed in a god who had allowed her to endure so much pain, or if she had become a good actress.

Did she only profess her faith because she knew John and Brenna were good Christians, or did she really believe the words she spoke? Had she been able to block out the ugliness of riding with Caleb Tyler and hold on to her faith? Somehow, he tended to believe she only gave lip service to the words to win over John and Brenna. For him to believe the words of a Tyler was too much of a barrier to overcome.

It was an unusually quiet Friday evening. By this time of night, he usually expected at least one fight at the tavern. For some reason, it didn't surprise him when Quaid McPhearson rushed into his office, out of breath. He smelled of whiskey and cigars. From the look on Quaid's face, Russ knew there had been trouble.

"What's wrong, Quaid?" he said, before the young man could say anything.

"You'd best come out to the farm, Russ. There's gonna be trouble. One of the Tylers just left the tavern."

Russ took a deep breath. "Are you certain? What did he look like? What kind of a horse did he ride?"

"He carried a pearl handled colt with a 'T' carved on it, just like the one Jesse carried. I couldn't tell you what he looked like, though. He wore his hat pulled down over his eyes the whole time. I can tell you he had a stubbly beard. If I hadn't seen the gun, I would never have known him. As for the horse, he rode off before I got outside."

Russ clasped his hands in front of him and stared ahead, remembering Jesse's words. 'Think back, didn't you see an old hermit, or perhaps a preacher man, or maybe just a drifter? Someone with an unkempt beard, someone who looked like he belonged and yet seemed somewhat foreign?'

Russ took little time in closing up the office for the night and mounting up to follow Quaid to the farm. His anger with Quaid boiled, but his concern for the safety of Jesse and the McPhearson family overshadowed it. His unexplained concern for Jesse baffled him, and yet he felt comfortable with it. Although he didn't want to care, he found he couldn't help himself. She seemed so small and helpless he worried about her safety. He never expected any of the Tyler gang to return for her. He wondered what he would find when he arrived at the farm.

"Did you talk to him?" Russ said, once they were on the road out of town.

"Not really, but everyone at the tavern wanted to know about Jesse. I guess I said more than I should have."

"Said more like what?" Russ pressed.

"Like Jesse was just about the most beautiful girl I'd ever laid eyes on. Like Brian's gone sweet on her, and she hangs on his every word. Like she's going to be out at the farm for a good spell yet."

"Did he have any idea who you were?"

"Don't see how he couldn't. Several people called me by name. If he gets anywhere near the farm, he'll see the sign Pa put up."

Russ rode in silence. To say anything now would be foolish. He knew he'd be unable to contain his temper. Instead, he dwelled on the things Quaid had said. Brian had gone sweet on Jesse and she on him. He wondered why that should bother him. He couldn't be falling in love with Jesse Tyler. Still, he couldn't deny the feelings he'd been having ever since the first time he met her.

She was too young, and she was a Tyler. She certainly wasn't anything like Ellie. He was a fool to think he could ever come to care for her.

* * * *

A faceless member of the Tyler gang leaned over Jesse as she slept. Russ pulled his gun before entering the downstairs bedroom of the McPhearson farm.

"You're under arrest," he said, his voice sounding strange in his ears. Before he could say more, the man pulled his gun from its holster and a single shot sounded.

Russ jumped, awakening himself in the process. The grandfather clock chimed five times, and he cursed himself for falling asleep when he'd come to keep watch over Jesse. He remembered the clock striking four as well as chiming four-thirty, and decided he hadn't slept long.

Getting up, he stretched and then looked through the open door to see Jesse still sleeping peacefully.

He wished Quaid had been more observant so he could have given a more accurate description of the man in the tavern. Had it been Frank? He doubted it. Frank would be relieved to think Jesse dead. No, it had to be Gary. Jesse called him her protector.

From his vantage point in the parlor, Russ could watch Jesse while she slept, unaware of his presence. She'd been asleep by the time he arrived at the farm. He and he alone made the decision to stand guard outside her open bedroom door, hoping the stranger would think her unattended and tip his hand.

He wondered what would happen if Quaid had been mistaken and no member of the Tyler gang came to her bedroom. What would he say to her? How would he explain his presence at this hour of the morning?

The lamp still burned beside Jesse's bed. In the flickering light, she looked more like an innocent child than a member of the notorious Tyler gang. Her red hair spread across the pillow, and her lips were parted, as she moaned softly in her sleep. He wondered if she could be dreaming and if those dreams were peaceful, or filled with the fear she had of Caleb and Frank.

These feelings for Jesse weren't right. At his age, he was much too old for her. She had a natural fear of him. He saw it in her eyes whenever they were alone. She had only just begun to trust him, but how would she feel when he arrested the stranger who will eventually come to find her?

* * * *

Russ held out his arms, and Jesse ran to their comfort. "I love you, Jesse."

"I love you too," she whispered back. He held her more tightly, and she enjoyed the security of his embrace.

"You know a lawman can't love a Tyler, Jesse Girl," Caleb said. "What about that faith in God you put so much stock in. This man has already told you he don't believe. Ain't it important anymore?"

She turned to face him and felt Frank's grip on her arm, pulling her away from Russ. "Pa's right, Jes. No lawman can ever love a Tyler. He's only using you to get us."

Without warning, her father pulled his gun and pointed it at Russ' heart.

She felt a callused hand cover her mouth and instantly the dream faded into startling reality.

"Jes, Jes, wake up, it's me."

38

Recognizing Gary's soft voice, she relaxed. She knew her gesture gave Gary the confidence to take his hand from her mouth.

"Gary? How did you find me?"

"It don't matter, Jes, we're gettin' out of here. I won't let them hang you. Now get up."

"You don't understand, Gary. I can't get up. I haven't been out of this bed since I got shot."

"Then I'll carry you. We gotta get away from here. I'm gonna take you with me. We'll head out for California or Oregon. We'll be safe there. No one knows us in those parts of the country. We'll change our names and start a new life. We won't have to be afraid of a rope anymore."

Jesse wondered how she could ever convince Gary she no longer had a fear of dying at the end of a rope. "I'm safe, Gary. God has saved me. He allowed these people to find me when I needed their help. He's sent the sheriff out here to tell me I'm not wanted, I'm not going to hang. Don't you see, He's saved you, too. He got you away from Pa and Frank and He's led you to me."

Before she could say more, Russ entered the room, his gun drawn. "Gary Tyler, you're under arrest."

Instinctively, Gary's hand went for his gun, but Jesse reached out to stop him. "Don't Gary. It's all right, the nightmare of riding with Pa is over. I'm free, and you'll be free too. Russ will see to it you get a fair trial."

"Russ?" Gary questioned.

Jesse nodded toward the man by the door and the lawman that held his gun unwaveringly.

"Who's with you, Gary?" Russ demanded.

"No one. They all think Jes is dead. They're all in Mexico," Gary replied, his voice shaky.

"Who shot Jesse?" Russ said.

"Jed Morris." Gary moved his hand again toward his gun.

"Give me your gun," Jesse pleaded. "Russ ain't gonna hurt you, I promise."

Carefully, Gary unbuckled his gun belt and handed it to Jesse. The weight of it took most of her strength, and she let it drop on to the bed.

"How did you know Gary would come here?" She spoke to Russ, unable to understand his presence.

"I stopped in town last night," Gary said, before Russ could speak. "I went to the tavern and found myself listening to some young buck spoutin' off about you, but I didn't think anyone recognized me."

Jesse turned toward Russ, as he picked up the gun belt from the bed. "This gave you away," he said, pulling the pearl handled colt from its holster. "It's the perfect match to the one your sister carried."

Jesse nodded. The one thing both she and Gary despised the most had trapped him. With the last of her quickly draining strength, she tried to show Gary everything had a meaning. "You'll see, Gary," she finally said. "God sent you here for a reason. Just trust in God and everything will work out, I promise."

"Trust in God, Jes? I don't think so. I tried trusting in God six years ago and it didn't work out then. You're safe and being cared for, nothing else matters."

Gary's words tore at her heart. Why couldn't he see things the way she did? Why couldn't he believe? "But Gary—"

"No, buts Jes," Gary said, touching her hand. "It's over. I can take anythin' knowin' you're safe and neither of us will ever have to face Caleb or Frank again."

Russ moved around to the other side of the bed and grasped Gary's arm. "Let's go," he ordered, his voice sounding cold and harsh.

Jesse cringed at the words, but couldn't find the strength to protest. Russ promised Gary a fair trial, God had brought Gary to her side. She had to trust in the Lord. Things would work out for the best. God wouldn't have brought them this far to have everything end in a disaster.

Chapter Seven

The days after Gary's arrest were draining for Jesse. The loss she experienced when Russ took Gary away was replaced by the exertion of getting out of bed.

On the following Monday, Dr. Page brought out a wheelchair and expected Jesse to use it. At first, she rebelled at the idea. Spending her life in a chair on wheels terrified her, and she protested violently.

"If you don't get up," Brian finally told her, "you won't be able to attend Gary's trial."

"If they have a trial," she replied without looking into Brian's eyes.

"Russ gave you his word, didn't he?"

"The word of a lawman. Do you think I should believe him? I mean he used me to trap Gary and see another Tyler hang."

As soon as she uttered the hurtful words, she regretted them. God brought her to the McPhearson household, just as he brought Gary to the same location. By not believing Russ, she was turning her back on God. Even if Russ didn't believe, she knew God worked through him and used him as a vessel to save her life.

"There's no use in fighting about this," she said. "I won't know if sitting in this chair will give me back my strength if I don't try."

Brian smiled and effortlessly picked her up and carried her across the room to the waiting chair. To her surprise, he bent and brushed his lips across hers before he put her down.

Fear radiated through her body as though the kiss had come from Ruben or Jed. "Why did you kiss me?" she said, when she regained her composure.

Brian began to smile broadly. "I couldn't help myself. You looked so beautiful, kissing you became a temptation I didn't want to resist. I could easily fall in love with you."

"No you couldn't, Brian," she said, sadly. "I couldn't let you. It wouldn't be fair."

"Why not?"

"Because Caleb would always be a threat. As long as he's free, I can never allow myself to love anyone again. It's too dangerous."

"But he thinks you're dead. Your brother said so."

"Maybe he does now," she began, trying to choose her words so as not to hurt Brian's feelings. "Who knows what will happen in the future. I can't just blend in with people. My hair and eyes would give me away in a minute. No one in their right mind would want to love me."

She prayed what she said would discourage Brian. She couldn't come out and tell him she didn't have the same feelings for him as he did for her.

Brian nodded. His expression told her the words hurt him. Without further conversation, he wheeled her chair into the kitchen.

"No more meals in bed," Brenna announced. "From now on you'll be coming to the table. Of course, being up will mean you'll be needing some proper clothes. I altered two of my old dresses for you. I hope you don't mind hand-me-downs, but I haven't had time to do any real sewing."

Jesse accepted the dresses from Brenna and ran her fingers over the delicate stitching. The dress reminded her of the ones she had made for Senora Mendoza and Carmalita. Just holding it in her hands reminded her of the dress Senora Mendoza gave her to wear. She had gone back to the shack, excited to put it on and feel like a woman again. When she arrived, Caleb ripped it from her hands.

"A Tyler don't take no charity from strangers," he had barked.

"Is it right to take their money at gun point, but not to take something we deserve? I've worked hard for Senora Mendoza. She gave me the dress as a gift."

Her comment ended when Caleb slapped her so hard she lost her balance. She never knew what became of the dress, but she assumed Caleb took it to the bordello in the next town. She would have bet anything Caleb gave it to Isabella and told her how he bought it for her.

"Is something wrong, dear?" Brenna said.

For the first time, Jesse realized she was crying. "No, nothing is wrong. I just remember the last time someone gave me a dress. Pa wouldn't let me keep it. He said the Tylers don't take charity from anyone. How can a gift, given in friendship, be charity?"

Brenna looked at her strangely. "You're right, of course, a gift given in friendship is definitely not charity."

Jesse clutched the dress tightly, pleased with the gift. Somehow, she would have to find a way to repay her debt to the McPhearsons.

* * * *

The warmth of the October sunshine beat on Jesse's face when she woke from her nap. She smiled at the knowledge she'd fallen asleep on the back porch of the McPhearson home, sitting in the wheelchair. In her lap lay her sewing. The emerald green and white calico fabric on which she worked would soon be a dress for her to wear to Gary's trial.

She heard voices from inside the house, but paid little attention. Surely, the McPhearsons had guests, and their identity would be none of her business.

"Where is she?" Jesse heard someone say. She wondered if she were dreaming, or if the voice actually belonged to her Aunt Hattie.

"She's out on the porch, but I think she has fallen asleep," Brenna replied.

The back door opened and, to Jesse's delight, her aunt and uncle joined her on the porch.

"Jesse, Jesse, dear, can it possibly be you?" Hattie cried, as she hurried to kiss Jesse's cheek.

"Oh, Aunt Hattie, how did you find me? How did you know just how much I needed to see you?"

"The McPhearsons wired us. We took the first train we could get to come to you," David replied.

Jesse looked up, accusingly at John and Brenna. "I thought I said—"

"What you said and what you meant were two entirely different things. Even if you couldn't see it, we could. We knew you needed the security of your family during this trying time." John and Brenna went back into the house, leaving Jesse alone with David and Hattie.

"Uncle David, they've captured Gary. Everyone assures me there will be a trial, but I haven't seen him since they took him away. I'm so frightened for him."

"Trust in the Lord, Jesse," David said. "He touched the hearts of the people here. Gary is safe, and there will be a trial. As you know, I practiced law before I received my calling from the Lord. I plan to use my knowledge to help your brother. A judge will be arriving on Wednesday, and the trial is scheduled for Thursday. God won't let anything happen to Gary."

"Even if he doesn't believe?" Jesse said, almost afraid of the answer. If Uncle David knew Gary was a non-believer, would he turn his back on her brother and return to Clarkston without waiting for the trial?

"Even if he doesn't believe," David answered, the softness of his voice putting Jesse at ease. "Gary has a good heart, and God will protect him. For now, we want to know about you. We didn't know what we would find, especially since Sheriff Martin told us how badly you were injured."

"I still can't walk alone, but Dr. Page assures me sitting in this chair will increase my strength more than staying in bed."

"You look so thin," Hattie interrupted. "I'm certain your father didn't take care of you properly."

Jesse sighed. She didn't know if she could tell her aunt and uncle about the horrors of riding with Caleb, about the beatings, the nights when the men hadn't left enough food to satisfy her hunger, about how she prayed to be saved.

"During the winters, I ate better than I did on the trail," she confessed. She continued to tell them about how she worked for the Mendoza family and how well she had been treated in their household. Before she knew it, words began spilling out of her mouth. Words, which made Aunt Hattie cry and Uncle David, shake his head in dismay.

"I know what you've told us couldn't have been easy for you," David said when she finished. "Still, it's something we needed to know. It will help me to defend Gary better. Are you willing to tell your story one more time?"

"Do you mean will I testify in court to help Gary? Of course, I will. I can't imagine doing anything less. Gary has been my protector, my confidant for too many years for me not to want to be there for him."

"Oh, David," Hattie lamented, "You can't be serious. Jesse is in no condition to go through such an ordeal."

Jesse smiled and shook her head. "You don't understand. No ordeal on earth could ever match riding with Caleb Tyler and watching the things he and Frank did. No matter what, I have to be at Gary's trial. I have to tell people the truth about what we suffered."

Chapter Eight

The morning of Gary's trial dawned ominously. Fog shrouded the entire Loveland area.

"It must be a sign," Hattie said. "I know it is. Jesse shouldn't be going."

Before Jesse could reply, support came from a strange quarter. "Of course she should be going," Quaid declared. "You're not going to stop her and neither is anyone else."

Jesse had been aware of the growing friendship between Gary and Quaid. Every day since Russ took Gary into custody, Quaid rode into town and spent time with him to get to know him.

"Well, Jesse," Quaid began, turning to face her, "are you ready to go?"

"Just about. I want to check my hair one more time." Picking up the hand mirror from the table, she looked at her reflection again. Aunt Hattie had brushed her hair one hundred strokes until it glistened. The green calico dress, the exact shade of her eyes, complemented her coloring perfectly.

Brian and John carried the chair out to the wagon as Quaid gently lifted Jesse into his arms. "It won't be easy," he said. "Gary's worried about you, but you'll show him. You'll show them all. You're stronger than you look."

"Thank you, Quaid. I never expected—"

"You don't have to say it," Quaid interrupted her. "You never expected me to care. At least not after the way I treated you when they first brought you here, when Gary first came. It's what you and Gary have done for me. Gary opened my eyes about a lot of things. When this

46

is all over, I'm going to strike out on my own for a while. Brian's the farmer, not me. Maybe I'll join the army."

"And fight Indians?" Jesse teased.

"At least fighting is something I've had some practice at. Lord knows I fight with my folks and Brian enough about my drinking."

"You said it, Quaid, not me," she replied.

"Like I said before, I've learned a lot from you and Gary. I need to grow up like you did."

"No one should grow up like we did. I know what you're trying to say though." She touched his cheek lightly with her finger and hoped the gesture wouldn't be taken in a way it wasn't intended.

Brian sat in the wagon, the chair secured in its bed. Quaid lifted Jesse to the seat next to Brian before climbing up to sit on the other side of her. It felt good to be out of the house and preparing to go into town, even though the reason for the trip was one that upset to her. Behind them, John held the reins of the team David rented. He'd be following his sons with Hattie and Brenna.

As they drove into town, Brian and Quaid made small talk, while Jesse remained lost in her own thoughts. It had been several days since she'd last seen Gary. Would he be surprised at the change in her appearance and the strength she'd gained?

As they pulled into town, the sleepy farming community Brian and Quaid described to her seemed to have disappeared. People milled everywhere. Men dressed in suits, cowboys, farmers, even women dressed in their best, stood in groups talking or making their way to the tavern. It looked like this would be a big day.

She remembered the courthouse had no building of its own. Quaid had told her the trial would be held in the tavern. She strained to make out the different buildings in the fog. Although the jail looked no different from the buildings on either side of it, just seeing where Gary had been held made her shiver.

"Will I get to see Gary before..." Jesse's voice dropped, unable to finish the question, unable to say the word trial.

"I doubt it," Brian said.

She wondered if it were her imagination, or had Brian changed over the past few days. It seemed as though Brian and Quaid exchanged places. Quaid now was concerned, and Brian only wanted this to be over. She knew he'd been hurt when she insisted they remain just friends.

Quaid squeezed her hand reassuringly.

Once they stopped the wagon, Jesse heard someone yell, "That's them, the folks who've been keepin' that Tyler gal."

"Can't understand why we ain't havin' two trials," someone else said. "One fer her and one fer him."

Jesse clenched her teeth and tensed as Quaid gently lifted her down and set her in the chair Brian and John had taken from the wagon.

"She's a looker," a man observed, as he stepped in front of her. Leaning close to her face, he continued. "You rode with them, how many people did you shoot? How many did you kill?"

"STOP IT!" she screamed. "I never killed anyone and neither did my brother."

"You're a Tyler," another man shouted. "We all know what the Tylers are. I watched the Tylers ride into my town and shoot my best friend. Left him a cripple for life, like you."

Someone else came forward with a rope tied into a crudely fashioned hangman's noose. "Got a rope right here. We could lynch her now and save us all a lot of time and trouble."

"That's about as far as you're going, Mister," John said, his voice cold and hard. "Now let us pass."

The crowd parted as Quaid wheeled Jesse's chair toward the tavern. David waited for them at the door. By the expression on his face, it was apparent he'd seen and heard the confrontation.

"Gary wants to see you privately, Jesse," he said, taking the chair from Quaid and pushing her toward a door on the other side of the room.

* * * *

Russ watched as Gary paced nervously, waiting for Jesse. "What if she doesn't come?" he said. "What if once I tell her the truth, she doesn't want to testify for me?"

"She'll be here," Russ assured him. "Try to relax."

"Relax? How do you expect me to relax? When this is all over, I know they'll hang me. Then what will become of Jesse?"

Russ took a deep breath. "No matter what the outcome—"

Before he could finish, the door opened and David wheeled Jesse into the room. Both Russ and Gary were taken aback. Jesse looked beautiful, more radiant than just a matter of days earlier.

Gary hurried to her side. Kneeling beside her chair, he hugged her. "Jes, I knew you'd come and yet I thought maybe you wouldn't. I'm having second thoughts. Maybe it's best..."

For an insane instant, Russ wished he were the one kneeling at Jesse's side. He shook his head to rid himself of the unexpected emotion. Jesse Tyler was and always would be Caleb Tyler's daughter. He couldn't lose sight of the fact. It wouldn't be fair to Ellie."

Jesse cringed a bit at Gary's words, then put her hand on his face and interrupted him. "Best what? Best if I go away? Best if I don't help you? No, Gary, I won't leave you to face this alone."

Gary smiled, reassured for the moment. "You look beautiful, Jes. I've never seen you look so pretty."

"You've never seen me in a dress, and I've never seen you look so tired," she replied, holding his hand. "Haven't you had any rest?"

"A little. I'll be all right." Gary paused, making Jesse wonder what he was leaving unsaid.

"There are some things you ought to know," Russ said. "There was a lynch mob last night."

Jesse tried to hold back the tears threatening to spring to her eyes, as her free hand covered her mouth.

"Many times during the night I wished they would lynch me, only they didn't," Gary confessed. "Now I'm here with you and relieved Russ wouldn't let it happen. I wanted to talk to you before any of this starts. There are some things David thinks you should hear from me, before you hear them in there." He paused, pointing toward the door.

"What would I not know? I lived it for three years." She watched as his eyes darkened and his brows knotted, the way they always did when he had something weighing heavily on his mind.

"You weren't going to be Ruben's woman," he said, flatly. "Jeb's either, if the truth be known."

"What? What are you saying? Do you mean he would have let me go free?"

"Not free, Jes. You weren't going to be Ruben or Jeb's woman, because Pa planned to sell you to the bordello. I've known it since before we rode north this spring. It's the reason I insisted you leave."

Jesse sat, shocked. Momentarily, she remained unable to speak. Gary couldn't be right. She would have known.

When she found her voice, she managed to speak. "You knew?"

"Yes. I figured you'd best know it now, because it's something we're gonna tell 'em."

"Why didn't you tell me?" she cried, her tears flowing rapidly.

"I hoped Caleb would change his mind and let Ruben or Jeb have you. Then I heard him talking to Ruben. Even if Ruben didn't understand his words, I did. I knew he would never change his mind, so I made certain you left."

Jesse pulled her hand away from Gary's grip. She had trouble believing what he'd just told her, even had trouble allowing him to touch her, considering he'd known about this. "I just can't understand why you didn't tell me?"

"What you were imagining about Ruben and Jeb seemed terrible enough, but it was much better than what your life in the bordello would have been."

"How did you know? I can't believe Pa told you."

"Of course, he didn't. He took me there. He bought me a woman."

"And you used her?"

Jesse's mind spun. How could Gary have gone to a place like Isabella's? How could he have taken a woman, like the ones who occupied the upstairs bedrooms?

"I thought you were different. I didn't think you were like them, but you are." Her accusatory words tasted like bile on her lips.

"I didn't use her, Jes. I didn't want anything to do with her, but she made me stay and made me listen to her. She told me what Pa planned to do with you." For a moment, a stony silence hung between them.

"And you believed her? You believed a woman like her?"

"She's the only sincere person I'd talked to in six years with the exception of you. Yes, I believed her. It wasn't hard to believe her. She was beautiful and her concern for you seemed genuine. She wasn't ashamed of her life, like we are. She didn't want you hurt. She knew what her kind of life would do to a Gringo."

"How could she be so certain?" Jesse pleaded, anger already seeming to give way to semi-belief. As the shock of his words sank in, she realized her father had intended to sell her, perhaps even make money off her for the rest of her life.

"Jesse," Russ said, breaking into her thoughts. "Clay predicted what would happen to you three years ago. He said Caleb would sell you in Mexico if you weren't already dead. He said a redhead would bring a good price down there."

"Clay? Clay knew, too?" she said, shocked at Russ' words.

"Clay guessed. He didn't know," Gary assured her. "None of us knew what would happen from day to day. Since we've brought it out in the open, do you want to change your mind. You can, you know. I wouldn't hold it against you. You don't have to testify."

"You know I don't," she replied, her tone softening, as she addressed her brother.

Reluctantly, she began to tell him of her encounter with the men in the street. Gary held her tightly as she sobbed.

"Why can't we be happy?" she said, through her tears. "Why can't we just go back to being children? Why can't we go home?"

"I don't know if we were ever happy, Jes. Maybe we just imagined what we thought to be happiness with Ma. It was a rough life, and it got rougher whenever Pa came home."

"It's time, Gary," David said, putting his hand on Gary's shoulder. "I think it would be best if Jesse sits next to you during the trial. It will ease her mind and give her comfort to be close to you."

David opened the door and Gary pushed Jesse's chair into the packed room. As they entered, all conversation ceased, all eyes turned to see the hated Tylers.

* * * *

"All rise, this court is now in session," Russ announced, as Judge Stover entered the room. Everyone but Jesse stood until the judge took his seat.

The jury of twelve men had been assembled earlier. Jesse wondered if they hated Gary as much as the men in the street hated her. Would they be fair? Would they listen? Would the defense fall on deaf ears?

"Gary Tyler," Judge Stover said, as Gary got to his feet. "You are accused of bank robbery and murder. How do you plead?"

Jesse watched Gary's face, as he hesitated only a moment. "I rode with them on the jobs, and I benefited from the money they stole, but I never killed anybody."

Jesse clung tightly to Gary's hand as the witnesses against him took the stand. Most of them were from small cattle towns whose names were unfamiliar to her. The first witness came from Stillwater in Oklahoma Territory.

"State your name, please," Emil Fink, the lawyer acting as prosecutor, said.

"Levi Abbott. I'm the owner of the bank in Stillwater."

"What happened in your bank when the Tylers came to town?"

The banker's eyes were so full of anger Jesse shuddered with fear. "They rode into town one morning. They robbed my bank. The sheriff over there can testify to it," he said, pointing to Russ. "When they left, his wife lay dead in the street, and he'd killed Ed Tyler in the bargain."

A knot formed in Jesse's stomach, as she looked at Russ. Why he'd gone to Slack Creek to talk to Clay had been a mystery until this moment. Russ went there for the same reason these people came to Loveland, to see a Tyler hang. Why Clay thought he could trust him and could tell him about her existence, she couldn't understand. Russ talked about an old debt, a phrase that meant nothing to her until now. Did Russ tell Gary about his wife? If so, why hadn't he told her? Why oh why, had he been so eager to come to the defense of a Tyler? Her father and brothers killed his wife. He should hate them.

"Were any of the other Tylers captured?" Emil continued.

"No, the others all got away, like they always get away. They got away with murder."

David began to question the man. "How many Tylers rode into Stillwater that day, and what year did you say this occurred?"

"There were five of them, and it was 1880, seven years ago."

David held up his hand and began to count on his fingers. "Let's see, Caleb, Frank, Ed, Will, and Clay, that's five men. Those were the same five men who rode together seven years ago. As a matter of fact, Gary Tyler still lived at home with his mother and sister in Clarkston,

Nebraska at the time. I don't see where any of this testimony is admissible because Gary Tyler has never been in Stillwater."

"He's one of them, same as the girl," Levi protested.

"Yes, they are Tylers, but Gary committed no crime in Stillwater. You are excused, Mr. Abbott."

It went the same with each man who testified. Caleb, Frank, Ed, Will, and Clay all committed murder, but no one could ever recall seeing Gary fire his drawn gun.

Tom Claxton from Slack Creek took the stand. As soon as he stated his name and where he came from, Jesse's stomach began to churn, her head spin.

"What happened in your town?" Emil prompted.

Tom took a deep breath. "It was June the sixteenth, three years ago. Six of them rode in and entered the bank. Caleb, Frank, Will, and Clay made no attempt to hide their identities, the other two wore masks. Someone in the bank pulled a gun and shot Will and Clay. They say one of the masked ones started to holler and Caleb told Frank 'to get that fool out of here.' Then they rode out of town. Will was dead before anyone could get to him. Clay was wounded. I took Clay into custody and after a fair trial he was hanged. Two people in our town died, four more were injured. I think I hit two of them as they rode away."

Tears rolled down Jesse's cheeks as she remembered Slack Creek. The memory of the morning was so vivid she could hear the shots. In her mind, she could see Will fall to the floor dead. She could feel Frank's grip on her arm as he pulled her from the bank, and she could hear her own screams. Vividly, she remembered riding until she ached and seeing the wounds her father and Gary suffered. She cringed as she recalled the crack of Frank's bullwhip.

By noon, the testimony against Gary ended and Judge Stover called for a recess. Again, Gary and Jesse were taken, with the Longs, McPhearsons, and Russ, to the room where they'd talked earlier.

As Aunt Hattie and Brenna put out the food they'd packed, Jesse's anger began to rise. How could they expect her to eat after hearing everything the men in the courtroom said?

"How can you set out dinner like nothing has happened?" she yelled.

Both Aunt Hattie and Brenna turned. Their faces denoted their horror at her words. They were women who had been trained to carry on, no matter what. Keep the house, feed the family, don't question.

Jesse's anger turned to Russ. "You're as bad as all the rest. You let me think you were different, but you ain't. You went to Slack Creek to see Clay hang, to get revenge. You even killed Ed. I know now, you made me feel safe just to get at Gary to satisfy yourself. Why don't you just let them hang us and stop wasting everyone's time with this mockery you call a trial?"

"Jes!" Gary shouted over her ranting. "Settle down. You ain't heard nothing you didn't know, except Pa and the others killed Russ' wife and Russ' bullet killed Ed. You had to know he went to see Clay hang. Now pull yourself together and eat something. You'll need all the strength you can get this afternoon."

Russ knelt by her chair and tried to console her. "You're right, Jesse. I did go to get revenge and see a Tyler hang. I don't know why Clay trusted me with the information about you. I'd like to think he thought I'd be able to help you some day. I tried to forget I'd ever heard the name Tyler, but I couldn't. I honestly do plan to help you."

For the first time, Russ held her close, allowing her tears to be absorbed by his shirt. She wished the moment would never end, wished he could hold her in his arms forever. As soon as the thought crossed her mind, she knew how ridiculous it seemed. Earlier this week, she'd questioned whether she could ever allow any man to touch her, now she sought the safety of Russ's arms. She knew, without a doubt, no man, certainly no lawman, could love a Tyler and no Tyler had the right to want it to happen.

* * * *

At last, the time came for Jesse to take the stand. Her stomach churned as David wheeled her chair forward. Before he turned her to face the packed room, Russ extended the Bible to her. Reverently, she put her hand on top of it and swore to tell the truth.

"I have no questions of this witness, Your Honor," David began. "I just want her to tell the court about her life riding with Caleb."

When the judge agreed, Jesse nodded. "I'm Jesse Tyler and I'm nineteen years old. I've been riding with Caleb for three years, I rode into Slack Creek with them. I was the fool who screamed. I never went with them into town again."

She paused long enough to let her words sink in. "Caleb thought having a woman with them would make his gang unique. He wanted me to ride as well as Gary, shoot as well as Clay, and be as ruthless as Frank."

David interrupted her with a question. "Did you live up to your father's expectations?"

Jesse again nodded. "Somewhat. I ride well, but I'll never equal Gary. If Clay were alive, a shooting contest would be a draw, but I'll never be like Frank. He enjoys inflicting pain and punishing whoever he feels deserves it. I wanted to get away from him, but until now, I've been too much of a coward to do anything but stay. I had nowhere to go, and Gary usually took my punishments for me. If I left, I knew his life would become a living nightmare at Frank's hands."

"To your knowledge, has Gary ever been guilty of murder?"

"I know he never killed anyone, because he can't pull the trigger."

Jesse could tell her composure came as a surprise to everyone, including Gary. Her voice didn't waver. The words she spoke told of her life as she lived it. It seemed as though she said, 'I learned to cook and sit with my sewing.' To her, the lifestyle she'd lived had become normal.

As the other attorney approached her, she vowed to stand up to his questions. She'd heard the things he'd asked Russ, questioned phrased to incriminate Gary.

"Miss Tyler, if you weren't taken into town, why didn't you leave when they were gone."

"At first Frank tied me hand and foot. When Gary protested, Caleb told me I had a price on my head. He led me to believe if I left, I'd be hanged. I didn't want to die. I'm not ashamed to admit I became afraid to leave. As added insurance I'd stay, they'd take my horse with them."

"Two weeks ago, you did leave them. What happened to bolster your courage now?"

"For three years, I'd worked as a seamstress in Mexico during the winters. It hadn't been a bad life. The money I made paid for the women and whiskey for Caleb and Frank. This summer it became clear either

Ruben Walden or Jeb Morris would take me as his woman when we got to Mexico. I couldn't stand the thought. I figured hanging would be better than being with one of them. I've since learned Pa never intended to give me to either of them. He'd made plans to sell me to a bordello."

Jesse watched the expressions on the faces of the people in the room. Women cried, men shook their heads in disbelief.

"You mentioned punishments. I'm certain these good people are like me, we all punish our children. It's how they learn. Don't you agree, Miss Tyler?"

For the first time, Jesse looked to Gary. He'd protected her from Frank's beatings, but he couldn't protect her from this. This time, she must fight her own battle.

"My father and brother's punishments are done with a bull whip," she said, as tears ran unbidden down her cheeks. "When we first left Mexico three years ago, Frank ripped off my shirt, tied my hands to a tree, and beat me because Will and Clay had been killed. He blamed me for their deaths. Gary usually took my beatings, but there were times when even he couldn't save me." Jesse looked at Gary and saw the hurt in his eyes.

"That's quite a story," the attorney sneered. "Of course, it's only your word. There are no other witnesses and I doubt we can believe a Tyler."

Jesse's anger overcame her composure. "I don't lie," she shouted. "I don't lie!"

"Stop it Jes," Gary said. Before he could get to his feet, David and Russ stopped him.

Jesse studied Gary's expression. His eyes, his expressive eyes, said the words she'd heard him voice so many times in the past. 'It's all right, Little One, I won't let anyone hurt you.'

Jesse regained her composure and sent a silent message of her own to Gary. Not this time, Big Brother. This time she had to take her own punishment.

Jesse turned back toward the judge. "I'm sorry, Your Honor," she said, her eyes lowered. She couldn't bring herself to make eye contact with the man. Even her voice betrayed the emotions raging within her. It sounded less confident, more strained, than before.

"Are you able to continue, Miss Tyler?" Judge Stover asked.

"Yes," she replied.

Emil again stood in front of her. "Just one more question. You indicated your brother never killed anyone. If you weren't with them all the time, how can you be so certain?"

"Caleb gave us each four gifts, a pearl handled Colt with a 'T' carved on it, a good Winchester, a horse, and a price on our heads. When I joined them, he made me strap on a gun and watch my brothers as they practiced. Frank and Will were good, they could hit the target, maybe not the bulls-eye, but they could hit it nonetheless. Clay never missed the bull's-eye, but Gary's shots were never true. Caleb told me Gary had been a disappointment, and he intended for me to be as good as Clay. I saw Gary's punishment for his wild shots, and I figured I'd show them and I did. By the time I left, I did the majority of the hunting for our food. Although Gary went with me, he never shot at anything. He'd get a rabbit or a deer in his sights and then put down the gun, unable to pull the trigger and end the life of a living thing."

Emil nodded. "I have no more questions for this witness, Your Honor."

David came forward and wheeled Jesse back to Gary's side.

"Would you like a short recess, Rev. Long?" Judge Stover said.

"No, Your Honor. It's best we finish what we've started. Gary and Jesse need to put this behind them and, whatever the outcome, get on with their lives."

Judge Stover agreed, and Gary took the stand. After being sworn in, he stated his name and age. Jesse wondered if the others in the room had as much trouble believing Gary to be only twenty as she did. His eyes betrayed his lack of sleep and his concern for her. He looked much older than his age. Perhaps he was older, not in years, but in experience.

Jesse listened to Gary's testimony and relived the past she so wanted to bury. Every word brought fresh memories of past injuries. She could see her mother taking to her bed for days after Caleb left. She could see Gary beaten and bleeding, but refusing to cry. She could see her father and brother fawning over their women, leaving her and Gary to work at menial jobs to support them.

She hardly realized Gary again joined her at the defense table;

hardly listened when Judge Stover adjourned the proceedings so the jurors could decide Gary's fate. She only came to full awareness when she and Gary were taken to the room where they had eaten dinner.

"What will you do, Jes?" Gary said.

"I haven't given it much thought," she sighed. "I guess I'll go back to Clarkston with Uncle David and Aunt Hattie. I can't stay here. The McPhearsons are wonderful people, but I won't continue to turn their lives upside down. David told me they never sold the farm. He's been renting out the land. He said he knew the Lord would bring me home. It's there for both of us. You've always wanted a horse farm. We could do it together."

"Slow down," Gary said, taking her hand in his. "Tomorrow may not come for me."

"Don't talk like this," she pleaded.

"Why not? We have to face facts. Neither of us knows what the jury will say. If we don't plan for the worst, it will be even harder if it happens.'

"You can't think this way. God won't let—"

A knock at the door interrupted her. "The jury has reached a decision, Gary," Russ said, as he entered the room.

Jesse could feel her face drain of color. She could feel her eyes fill with sadness and tears.

"Face it, Jes. Whatever happens in there, happens. I know they'll hang me. I didn't want to put it to you this way, but you have to be prepared for what will happen," Gary said, as he guided the chair through the open door.

* * * *

Russ tried to read the faces of those people around him, but couldn't. While they'd waited for the decision of the jury, a group of men, including Levi Abbott and Tom Claxton, asked to speak with the judge. Their request had been puzzling.

Behind him, John and David comforted their wives, who had been crying softly through most of the day. It seemed as though each woman planned to claim Gary and Jesse as her own. He was afraid the outcome of today's trial would shatter their lives forever.

Across the room, the jury returned to their seats. These were twelve men Russ had come to know well over the past three years, but their thoughts were unreadable. Their expressions were noncommittal, as though they had been carved in stone.

Now Jesse sat next to Gary, fear, anger, and despair radiating from her eyes. He wanted to hold her and comfort her, but he knew it wasn't right. He recalled the feel of her in his arms, just hours ago, and ached to hold her to protect her against the jury's verdict. He knew he'd never be her protector. Once the trial ended, whatever the outcome, David and Hattie were taking her to Clarkston. She'd disappear from his life as quickly as she'd appeared.

"Have you reached your decision?" Judge Stover spoke to the jury.

"We have, Your Honor," Eli Otto, an old farmer from south of town said.

Judge Stover turned his attention to Gary. "Gary Tyler, please rise and face the jury."

When Gary stood, Judge Stover addressed the jury. "To the charge of bank robbery, how do you find the defendant?"

Eli's eyes looked pained as he spoke. "Guilty."

"No," Jesse cried, releasing her grip on Gary's hand and covering her face.

Judge Stover rapped his gavel for silence, and Gary groped for Jesse's hand. The judge's voice remained emotionless as he spoke. "To the charge of murder, how do you find the defendant?"

The room became deathly quiet, as everyone held their breath in anticipation of the one word verdict.

Eli studied Gary. "Innocent."

Hattie and Brenna's tears of sadness became tears of joy, and Gary knelt next to Jesse. Russ watched as the tension of the day drained from her body and exhaustion began to set in.

Again the gavel sounded. "Gary Tyler, you have heard the verdict of the jury. You've been found guilty of bank robbery. During the deliberation of the jury, your accusers asked me to be lenient. I tend to agree with them. I can think of no punishment to equal the one you've already endured at the hands of your father. For the next five years, you'll report all of your activities to Sheriff Martin and receive the permission of the court if you plan to leave this area. Should these conditions not be met, you'll be sent immediately to the state penitentiary for the remainder of the five years. This court is dismissed."

Russ smiled at the bewilderment in Gary's eyes. "You're free to go, Gary," Russ shook Gary's hand.

"I can't believe it," Gary replied, as he accepted Russ' gesture of friendship, then hugged David, and turned to find Jesse, shakily trying to get to her feet. Before she could stand on her own, he pulled her into his arms, supporting her weight as she hugged him tightly.

As he lowered her back into the chair, Russ noticed Eli Otto standing behind Gary.

"Young man," Eli said, his German accent thick and noticeable. "During the trial, your sister said you know horses. I could use some help on my farm. I raise horses, but I'm an old man. I can no longer continue alone. Think about it, young man. Anyone can tell you where I live. Ride out on Monday and look things over. You can give me your answer then."

"Thank you, Mr. Otto. I'll be out to your place on Monday ready to work."

"Eli's an odd old duck," Russ said. "If you like horses, you'll enjoy working with him. He has a lot to teach a young man. Give him an honest day's work and he'll give you an education like you would get nowhere else. He has trouble getting good help. I think it's because he demands hard work and doesn't tolerate hard drinking."

"His conditions don't sound too harsh to me," Gary said. "The judge said five years. For those five years, I have to do something. Why not do something I enjoy?"

"I think you've got the right idea, Gary," Russ agreed. "Eli will be good to you if you treat him fairly."

Russ turned from Gary to say something to Jesse, but Quaid had already started to wheel her chair toward the door. Maybe that was for the best. She had a whole new life to build and he'd done what he told Clay he would do. He could go on and really start to live.

Before Quaid got Jesse to the door, Russ heard her laugh. He'd only heard her laughter once and then it hadn't contained the tinkling tone he heard now. A longing filled him as he realized he wanted to hear her laugh again, wanted her to be part of his life. Instead of going to her, he turned back toward the table where he sat most of the day. A few papers remained for him to pick up and take back to the office.

Best to let her go. Start over again. No Tyler was worth his concern. He'd done his best.

Chapter Nine

By Sunday, the weather grew colder, as a wind from the north set the tone for the coming winter. When the McPhearson household woke and prepared for church, winter descended upon them. A light dusting of snow on the barren fields made everything look clean and new.

Brenna and Hattie worked preparing breakfast for the overly full household, while Brian, Quaid, and Gary tended to the milking. In the front room, John and David talked, as usual, about the future Gary and Jesse could expect.

With breakfast finished, everyone started getting ready for church. It came as no surprise to Jesse when both Gary and Quaid declined to accompany them.

"But Gary," Hattie protested, "the Lord has saved you. Can't you find it in your heart to give him one hour of your time?"

As much as Jesse wanted Gary by her side in church, she knew he wouldn't relent. Perhaps he would never find the Lord. She prayed for it daily, but expected no immediate answers. She knew what Caleb had done to Gary and knew his acceptance would not come easily.

After church, Hattie and Brenna worked at warming the food and setting the table. By the time the men entered the kitchen and found their places, ham, scalloped potatoes, squash, rolls, and applesauce laced with freshly ground cinnamon graced the table. On the sideboard sat pumpkin, apple, cherry, and mince pies.

Jesse couldn't help but watch Gary. She'd become accustomed to such meals while living with the McPhearsons. She also knew what she and Gary were accustomed to for meals on the trail. It wasn't hard for her to see Gary was amazed by the amount of food spread before him.

After dinner, the men adjourned to the parlor to enjoy their cigars and pipes, while Brenna and Hattie cleaned up in the kitchen.

Feeling out of place in both situations, Jesse went to her room to lie down. She'd become determined to learn how to handle the wheelchair by herself and with great effort lay down on the bed.

She longed to sleep, to forget her confusing emotions. Brian had professed his love, had kissed her in a way she knew a dozen other girls wanted him to kiss them, and yet his kiss repulsed her. Brian's light and loving touch reminded her of Ruben's unwelcome advances.

On the other hand, Russ had never been improper, only held her to comfort her, and yet she longed to hear him say he cared for her. She knew how terribly wrong her thoughts were, but she couldn't help having them. Russ surely considered her little more than a child and worse yet, Caleb Tyler's child.

She fell asleep, wishing when she woke she would find Russ sitting across from her, yet knowing it to be an impossible dream.

Tomorrow she'd board the train with David and Hattie to begin her new life in Clarkston. Tomorrow Loveland and Russ would be left behind and somehow she would try to forget everything she'd experienced here.

* * * *

March, 1889

Russ waited for Gary in his office. On the fourth Saturday of the month, Gary came into town with Eli, collected his mail, and stopped at Russ' office. Hungry for news about Jesse, Russ looked forward to the monthly visits. Although he knew Gary distrusted him, perhaps even hated him, he appreciated every shred of news he had to impart.

Looking at the clock, he noticed it would soon be striking twelve. Maybe something had delayed Gary. He might not even be coming today. If he didn't, Russ knew he would have to make the trip out to the Otto farm to find out what happened. Monthly visits were one of the provisions of Gary's freedom. For some unknown reason, Russ didn't want to see the boy lose something so precious.

The chimes of the clock just began to strike when Gary entered the office. "I didn't think you were coming today," Russ greeted him, as they shook hands.

"Chores took longer than usual this morning," Gary replied, noticeably nervous about being late.

Russ wished Gary would be a little more at ease in his presence. It would be a plus if he could do more than make polite conversation and look like he wanted to bolt and run. He realized in the past months Gary had made many life changes.

"Did you hear from Jesse today?" Russ said.

As soon as he put voice to the question, he wondered why he asked it. He had no idea why she so intrigued him, why he wanted to hear everything about her, but he couldn't help himself.

"As a matter of fact, I did. I've got so much on my mind today, I forgot to mention it to you."

Gary fingered the letter in his pocket as if trying to decide how to tell Russ what it contained. The gesture gave Russ an uneasy feeling.

"Jes is leaving Clarkston right after Easter. She wants me to ship the gray to her so she can move on."

"Move on?" Russ echoed. "Where? Why? I thought she'd be staying in Clarkston and taking over the farm."

"I did too, but she's definitely not happy there. She wants to move to Denver and start a new life with a new name."

"I can't believe she isn't coming here to see you," Russ said.

"She said there were just too many bad memories here, you know, with the trial and all. We'll keep in touch. Maybe she'll even come back here some day."

Russ could feel his stomach start to churn. How could Jesse do such a thing to Gary? He protected her for years. She can't destroy him by not coming back to at least see him once more before she moves on.

"Don't ship the horse off until I have time to think things through. I have some time coming, maybe I can talk to her. It don't seem right, her not coming to see you."

Chapter Ten

Clarkston, Nebraska – March, 1889

Clarkston hadn't been the answer. Jesse knew it within the first few days of her arrival. With the exception of Walter Carson, she could never remember having friends in Clarkston, and, now, not even Walter seemed to be beating a path to the parsonage to welcome her back.

At first, she'd been content to sit in her chair, day after day, reading or sewing. It had been David who challenged her and made her want to walk again. At Christmas, he'd given her a pair of crutches and bullied her into using them. Now, three months later, she'd graduated to using a cane. Although her progress was steady, doubt and self-pity filled her private moments .

She'd thought a visit to the farm would bring some meaning to her life. David and Hattie had held onto the land for her, and perhaps God meant for her to begin her new life there. Against David's wishes, she drove the buggy out to the farm alone.

With the exception of the small piece of land where her mother and brother rested, she saw no sign of the horse or barn. The land had been plowed, planted, and harvested, but the ghosts who continued to haunt Jesse still lingered.

"No Caleb, not Gary," her mother had pleaded. "He ain't like the other boys, he's so young, and he's—"

"He's a Tyler, Laura. He's my son. I'll do with him as I see fit and you won't interfere." The sound of flesh striking flesh rang in Jesse's ears.

"Stop it! Stop it! Stop it!" she screamed.

When she opened her eyes, she stood alone in the small cemetery. She dropped to her knees beside her mother's grave, feeling the damp

March earth beneath her. She covered her face with her hands and began to sob. She could never return here. Although the land had been stripped of its former identity, her parents and brothers would always haunt her.

She couldn't stay here, she admitted to herself. She couldn't rebuild her life here. She'd never have the strength to rebuild the farm. Even if Gary came back, it would be too difficult.

At last, the tears stopped, and, with a feeling of peace, she silently communicated with her mother. She had to move on. There was nothing here for her. It was best if she got as far away from Caleb's territory as possible. With the things she'd learned from Aunt Hattie she could easily leave here and move further west. It would be easy enough to change her name and start a seamstress shop anywhere. Maybe even Denver. Everyone said it was a growing city. She could grow with it and lose herself in the process.

To her surprise, she felt someone touch her shoulder. Knowing she was alone, she turned abruptly, half expecting to find Caleb standing behind her.

"Is something wrong, Jesse?" Walter said.

Recognizing him, she relaxed and began to smile. "Nothing is wrong. I came out here to set my mind straight and to visit with Mama."

Walter helped her to her feet. As he did, she enjoyed the touch of his hand and remembered their stolen kisses when they thought no one was looking.

"I'm sorry I didn't come around sooner," Walter said. "You know how it's been with winter and all. I've been meaning to come in and see you. I've been meaning to come to church, too, but with the amount of snow we got this year, we couldn't get out. Then Ma took sick and, well, none of us have gotten much of anywhere."

Jesse's heart jumped at the thought of Walter wanting to see her. He did want to see her again. This could be his way of saying he wanted to start courting her.

"I wanted to see if we could strike a deal so I can use the land again this year."

The words Walter spoke silenced Jesse's inner voice. Disheartened, she took a moment to put her thoughts in order.

"Are you in a position to buy this land, Walter?"

"Well, yes I am. Suellen and I have talked about building a farm here. We got married last spring, and you know how it is livin' with your parents, but Rev. Long..."

Jesse cringed at learning about Walter and Suellen. How could she have thought he would have waited three years for someone who could be dead? Why hadn't anyone bothered to mention his marriage to her? Maybe they thought it would unduly upset her. She wanted to cry and lash out, but instead, she interrupted Walter before he could tell her anything more.

"If you want this land, I'll sell it to you right now. Just tell me what it's worth and we'll have a deal. I know you won't cheat me."

"Of course I wouldn't cheat you. I just don't understand this. How can you even consider selling the land?"

"I can't stay here," she replied. The joy at seeing Walter and thinking he might be interested in her left her voice. "They're here. Pa, Ma, the boys, their spirits are here. I could never live on this land, not even with a new house and barn. I don't know if I'll ever be strong enough to run a farm by myself."

Walter looked at the cane lying beside her on the grass and bent to retrieve it. She knew he must have heard how her father's men tried to kill her and left her a cripple. She also knew, he, like most people, found it almost impossible to believe.

"It won't be forever," he said, handing her the cane. "You'll get your strength back. You might even change your mind about this place."

"Nothing is forever, but I won't change my mind," she replied. "I thought riding with Pa would be forever, but it finally ended. I've come to grips with my feelings. I want to be shed of this place and all the memories it holds. I'll sell you this land. It's eighty good acres. With a dedicated farmer, it will more than pay for itself."

She watched Walter's expression and knew he could feel the hurt in her words. Selling the land had been a monumental decision, one she didn't make lightly. To her relief, he seemed to understand her motives.

"I've heard the stories of Gary's trial and of the life the two of you lived. It's no wonder the land haunts you. I can understand why you're so eager to sell it. That time must have been a nightmare. It makes me wonder what might have happened if you'd stayed in Clarkston instead of going away with your Pa."

"You make it sound like riding with him was my decision. I can assure you I fought him tooth and nail."

"I'm sorry, I didn't mean it the way it sounded."

"I know you didn't. If I hadn't been forced to go with Caleb, we would have been married with a house full of kids. Of course, I didn't stay in Clarkston and we didn't get married. All I want now is for you to tell me you will consider buying the land." She prayed she didn't sound too bitter about the past or too anxious about the future.

"I'll be in to talk to you about it," he promised, as he helped her get into the buggy. "I'll stop by the parsonage tomorrow, after I go to the bank."

"I'll look forward to seeing you." She watched Walter turn from her and mount his horse. At one time, her life revolved around being his wife. Now she wondered if she could ever be happy with a quiet steady farmer like Walter, when Russ Martin dominated her thoughts, her prayers, and even her dreams.

* * * *

After telling her aunt and uncle of her plans, the days passed quickly. Her decision to leave just after Easter gave her the strength to work harder to become independent.

Palm Sunday, with the message of the joyous entry and undertones of the events of the week to come, began Jesse's last week in Clarkston.

By Good Friday, she had begun to doubt her decision. If she didn't feel strong enough to run the farm, how could she start a new life?

Her doubts centered on Loveland as well. She wanted to see Russ, and yet she worried about such a meeting. To him, she'd been but a child, while to her, he'd become an impossible dream. She knew she needed more time before she could make a commitment, yet she longed to hear him say he cared for her. Silently, she cursed her obsession with what she could never have. Russ Martin had good reason to hate the Tylers, and she had good reason to dismiss him from her thoughts. He told her he didn't believe in God. How could she ever consider a life with anyone who did not share her faith in the Lord?

She realized she had no time for doubts. She had too many things to do before Sunday arrived. David had persuaded her to sing a solo at the Easter service. With everything else she had to do, she'd found time to spend at the piano, practicing with Hattie. Every time she thought she would never learn the piece, she remembered David insisting it would be a fitting parting gift.

* * * *

Russ sat on the train and brooded. How could Jesse cut Gary so short when she knew how much he loved her? How could she expect him to just ship her the gray and not see her? The questions without answers crowded his mind, making him more confused than ever about Miss Jesse Tyler.

All during the trip, Russ hoped he could persuade her to come back with him to Loveland. The closer the train came to Clarkston, the more doubts nibbled at his mind.

He wondered how he would approach Jesse once he arrived in Clarkston. Perhaps he should do as Gary suggested. What harm would it do to attend services on Sunday, sit at the back of the church, and watch her from afar? When Ellie died, he purposely put God out of his life, but in order to see Jesse, he needed to go to the church. He would have to be content to watch her from afar before seeing her face to face. The only place he could do that was in church. It's something that is important to her and would be the perfect place to be just one of the crowd.

He was the first to admit, Jesse confused him. Maybe he wanted her to confuse him. Did he think he could sweep her into his arms and kiss away three years of riding with Caleb? Had he built her up in his mind as a pure and innocent child, just because Clay told him as much? Did he want to punish her for what Caleb did to Ellie? He didn't know, and he wasn't certain he wanted to find out. He only wanted to tell her how selfish it is for her to go to Denver without seeing Gary again.

His inner ramblings ceased as he remembered how he felt when Gary told him of Jesse's plans to go to Denver and start a dress shop. If she goes to Denver, she'll have a new life with a new name. Would there be a place for him there? Would she even keep in contact with Gary? Could he let her slip away from him so easily?

The thought of her being so far away ate at him until he admitted he cared for her. He wished she would care for him, but he knew it was impossible. He was a lawman. He'd done nothing to warrant her affections. He'd touched the lives of three of her brothers in a negative way. Not only had he killed Ed and gone to see Clay hang, but he'd been the one to arrest Gary and put her through a grueling trial.

Russ forced himself to think of why he was making this trip. He'd considered every argument he could think of to persuade Jesse to return to Loveland. He'd even gone so far as to look at a small house at the end of Main Street. Loveland could use a dressmaker, and the house would make a perfect shop for her. Perhaps he could convince her life in Loveland, close to Gary, wouldn't be half-bad.

The train arrived in Clarkston late on Saturday evening. Russ easily found the boarding house across the street from the church.

By morning, he wondered why he'd bothered renting the room. Although he'd tried, sleep eluded him. Jesse dominated his thoughts, driving any thoughts of rest.

With the first light of dawn, he got out of bed and dressed. From his window, he watched as families entered the church. Seeing Jesse leave the parsonage, he held his breath. She looked as beautiful as he remembered. He hadn't seen her walk before, and although she did so with a cane, she carried herself well.

Once she entered the church, he left his room. When he slipped into the sanctuary, he saw Hattie sitting at the front of the church playing the piano. Just ahead of him, David walked down the aisle. He breathed a sigh of relief as he took a seat in the back pew. For the time being, no one had recognized him.

From his seat in the back, he halfheartedly listened to the service. A small choir, under Hattie's leadership, sang songs of praise as rays of sunlight streamed through the windows, highlighting Jesse's red hair.

Just after the sermon, Jesse stood, then began to sing. Russ listened, entranced by the fact Jesse's voice reminded him of the angels David talked about in his sermon. He could never remember hearing anyone with such a pure sweet voice.

Suddenly, the words of David's sermon, the words of salvation took on new meaning. It seemed as if God brought him here, intended for him to hear Jesse singing the words of praise.

Ellie, too, seemed to come to him. 'It's all right, Russ,' he could hear her say. 'It's time for you to begin to live again. Jesse is as pure and innocent as you imagine her to be. Take a chance. Find God again and put the past to rest. I only want your happiness.'

Russ shook his head to rid himself of the uninvited voice. He needed to concentrate on the things happening around him. To his amazement, the service had ended.

David stood to give the benediction, but before beginning he made an announcement. "There are hot cross buns and coffee at the parsonage for anyone who would like to stop by."

Around him, people murmured and nodded to one another as David gave the benediction. It took little time for the people to begin to leave.

Russ tried to concentrate, but he couldn't take his eyes off Jesse. He'd grown nervous about talking to her. He admitted to himself, for the first time, he'd come to Clarkston to plead his own case, not Gary's. When he'd heard Jesse wouldn't be coming to Loveland, he hadn't been able to stand not seeing her again. Perhaps his anger over Jesse not seeing Gary had prompted this trip, but he knew it was his own feelings, which made him come. Now, he wondered what would happen if she turned him down, if she said Denver was too important, or worse, if she considered him too old. What if she only wanted to disappear and never be found?

He watched the people continue to leave. At the front of the church, he saw a young man come up to Jesse and put his hand on her arm as they began to talk. Jesse's face brightened with a smile he could see even from her profile. He saw her laugh and remembered what her laughter sounded like.

Russ' heart skipped a beat and threatened to stop. He shouldn't have come. Jesse's life had continued. She'd found a young man, not much older than herself who could make her smile, make her laugh, make her happy. He doubted if he would ever be able to do those things.

This trip had been wrong from the start. He knew that now. He also knew he couldn't force someone to want him. With Ellie, everything had come naturally. With Jesse, he'd done everything wrong.

For the first time, he looked for another way out of the church, a way in which he could avoid shaking hands with David and being seen by Jesse. To his dismay, there appeared to be none.

He felt even more trapped when Jesse passed within feet of where he sat. Fear turned to gratitude, when she'd been so engrossed in her conversation with the young man she didn't notice him. He imagined the man helping her down the steps of the church, accompanying her to the parsonage, perhaps even sharing an intimate moment or a light kiss. He would never share any of those things with her.

He had to find a way out. He cursed himself for taking the train. Why hadn't he ridden? It would have taken longer, but it would have been worth it. If he had his horse here, he could wait until the church completely emptied, until David returned to the parsonage, and then leave for Loveland. Now, he would be forced to wait until morning for the next train.

To his surprise, it took very little time for the church to empty and leave him alone with his self-accusations. He'd gotten a reprieve after all. Gratefully, he leaned back against the pew and began to formulate a plan. He'd gotten so little sleep the past two nights, he'd go back to his room and sleep. Come morning, he'd board the train for Loveland and try to forget Jesse Tyler.

"Russ?" David's voice boomed from behind him. "Russ Martin? What are you doing in Clarkston?"

Russ turned to face David, realizing his reprieve had been short lived. "I had some time coming. Gary said Jesse would be leaving for Denver, and—"

"Jesse will be thrilled to see you," David interrupted, pumping Russ' hand.

"I don't think so. This has been a terrible mistake. Don't even mention you saw me."

"Nonsense, you come over to the parsonage with me right now," David ordered, his grip still firm on Russ' hand.

"It's best I be on my way," Russ protested. "I haven't had much sleep. I'll just go back to the boarding house and rest."

David's look seemed as firm as his grip. "You can rest later. Come over to the house. My life wouldn't be worth much if those two women didn't get to see you."

Russ saw no use in arguing. The trap he thought he'd successfully avoided seemed to be closing in on him.

"I suppose I don't have much choice in the matter. I'll stop by for a minute to see Hattie."

Reluctantly, he followed David to the parsonage, his stomach in knots. It appeared to be a comfortable home. Although he knew most of the furnishings were donations from the congregation, discarded pieces no longer needed in their homes, Hattie's flare for decorating made each piece look as though it had been carefully selected to fit perfectly into its assigned place.

He heard Jesse's voice, even though he couldn't see her. Maybe he still had a chance to get away before she knew he was here.

"Come with me, Russ. I know a young lady who'll be very pleased to see you," David said, leading him farther into the house.

"I'm sorry, David, I think I should go. Like I said before, this whole thing has been a mistake. I have to leave."

Before he could turn toward the door, Jesse came out of the kitchen, a plate of hot cross buns in one hand, and her cane in the other. She remained engrossed in conversation with another young woman. She hadn't seen him. He still had time to leave and yet he stayed, as though he'd become rooted to the spot.

She looked more youthful and more radiant, than she had just months earlier. Her eyes sparkled, her cheeks had color. He didn't want to be hurt and yet he couldn't leave. He couldn't go without talking to her one last time.

Jesse set the plate on the table. Looking up, she saw him standing there. Her face mirrored disbelief, then brightened as she smiled, the way she'd smiled at the young man in church. Russ looked around the room for the young man, but didn't see him. Could her smile be for him and not for the man she'd been talking with earlier?

Russ took a tentative step toward Jesse. "Hello," he said, taking her free hand in his.

"Hello, Russ. What are you doing here?" She spoke, apparently bewildered by his presence.

"I ... I guess I came to see you," he stammered.

"But I'll be in Loveland in two days. Why make such a long trip when you'll be seeing me in so short a time?"

"What?" He was shocked by her statement.

"Didn't Gary tell you? I have a ticket for tomorrow's train to Loveland. I planned to see you and the McPhearsons before I picked up the gray and took the train to Denver."

"Oh," Russ said, feeling silly for being there. Now more than ever he wanted to get away from the parsonage and away from Jesse.

"Gary didn't tell you, did he?"

"No. It's been good seeing you, Jesse, real good." He dropped her hand, embarrassed to be holding it and standing here looking at her like a lovesick schoolboy. He turned toward the door, but her hand on his arm stopped him.

"You're going to walk away, aren't you?" she said, her voice sounding as though he'd slapped her.

"I need some thinking time. Some time to figure out you Tylers. I don't understand any of you." He could no longer face her. He pulled away and headed toward the door.

Stepping into the bright sunlight of the unseasonably warm April morning, he heard her steps behind him. They sounded slower than his. He could easily outdistance her, but her voice again stopped him.

"I think we need to talk," she pleaded.

He turned back to face her, surprised to see tears in her eyes. Helping her down the steps, he escorted her to the double swing in the back yard and steadied it so she could sit comfortably.

Once he seated himself beside her, she asked the question he knew puzzled her. "Just what did my brother tell you?"

"He said you were going to Denver and changing your name. I guess I couldn't fault you for wanting to disappear. He also said you'd be opening a dress shop."

"And what else?" she demanded.

"He intended to ship the gray here and you weren't coming back to Loveland. He said you were willing to wait five years to see him."

"So you came here to plead his case. I don't know why, but he lied to you. I'm due to arrive in Loveland on Tuesday at noon."

"I think I know why," Russ confessed. "I guess I'm not very good at hiding my feelings. I care for you, Jesse. I know I shouldn't. Your father and brothers killed my wife. I should hate you for being who you are, but

I can't get you out of my mind. Gary must have known I couldn't let you disappear without seeing you."

"Is that why you came here?" Her bright smile accompanied her hopeful eyes l.

"I told myself I'd do this for Gary. I'd beg you to come to Loveland to see him. I guess I knew all along it wasn't for him. I should have known better than to believe such a cock and bull story. I don't know you well, but I do know you wouldn't disappear without seeing him first. I came to ask you to reconsider. I don't want you to go to Denver. I don't want to push you into anything you aren't prepared to handle either. All I'm asking is for a chance to get to know you." His eyes were locked on hers, his hand held hers firmly.

"Oh, Russ, I want to get you know you, too, but—"

"But what, Jesse?"

"I don't know if I can, since you don't want to know the Lord."

"I used to know Him. It seems like we had a falling out after Ellie died. This morning, hearing you sing in church, we started to renew our acquaintance. It will take time, but I think we can get together again. If I'm not mistaken, He's been trying to talk to me for a long time. I've just been too bullheaded to listen. There is one thing I have to know, though. After the service, I saw you talking to a young man. Is he ... I mean, I don't want to spoil things for you with him."

"You saw me talking to Walter Carson. A lifetime ago he wanted to marry me. Now we're just friends. I sold him the farm three weeks ago. He wanted to tell me how he and his wife, Suellen, are going to rebuild the house and barn. I plan to give Gary half the money, or at least try to, when I get to Loveland."

"Then why not stay close to him?" Russ said, desperate to understand her logic.

"Because I'm a threat to Gary in Loveland and to everyone I care for there," she replied, flatly.

"What do you mean? Help me to understand."

"How many young women do you know with bright red hair and emerald green eyes? Someday Pa will find me. I'm not like Gary. I can't just melt into the crowd. I cost him a lot of money and he'll—"

"He thinks you're dead, Jesse."

"Maybe, maybe not. I don't know. I do know Gary will blend in and fit in well. I'm just so afraid of what might happen to him if Pa ever finds me."

"I'll protect you."

"The way you did your wife? I doubt it. No one can protect me from Caleb Tyler. I'd like to think you would be able to do it, but I can't be certain. I need time to heal. Time to find out who and what Jesse Tyler is. I don't know if there really is a Jesse Tyler. Maybe it would be for the best if she died the way Pa wanted her to. I only know I have to have time to figure it all out, and I don't know if I can do it in Loveland."

"You can have all the time you need, all the time in the world, if I'd be able to come and visit you often so that I can get to know you. I can't do that with you in Denver. You need to be in Loveland for it to happen."

A long silence preceded her answer. "I guess you're right. I will come to Loveland and give it a try, at least for a few months. If nothing else, it will give me a chance to confront Gary. Mark my words, when I get my hands on my brother..."

Russ began to smile. "Don't be too hard on him. He only wanted to make me see how special you are."

He helped Jesse to her feet and then handed her the cane, which lay beside them in the grass. Just touching her hand reassured him and made him certain he done the right thing in coming to Clarkston.

Once inside the parsonage, David and Hattie greeted him warmly.

"It's good to see you, Hattie," he said, as he took her hand in his.

"It's good to see you as well," Hattie replied. "This certainly is a surprise. Come out to the kitchen. I'll get you something to eat.

"It sounds good. I guess I'd forgotten how hungry I am. There's been too much going on."

When they entered the kitchen, they found Belle Clark filling plates with hot cross buns. "Oh, Jesse dear," she oozed, with false sincerity. "You must introduce me to your friend."

"Mrs. Clark, Mrs. Belle Clark, this is my friend, Russ Martin." Jesse watched as Russ took Belle's hand.

"Hattie tells me you're a lawman," Belle said, her voice more sugar coated than Jesse could ever remember hearing it in the past. "It must be a really exciting vocation."

"I guess you could say it is. It's a pleasure to meet you."

"Oh, Marshal, the pleasure is all mine. I do hope our dear little Jesse isn't in any trouble with the law. Her life hasn't been an easy one, you know."

"It's Sheriff, Ma'am," Russ corrected her, "and no, Jesse isn't in any trouble with the law. Gary's been worried about her traveling alone. He asked me to escort her back to Loveland on tomorrow's train."

Belle's eyebrows shot up in surprise. From the look on Jesse's face, Russ suspected she knew the woman would like nothing better than to glean some damaging information she could pass along to anyone who would listen.

"Isn't that nice of you, taking time out of your busy schedule," she gushed.

"Gary would have come himself," Russ continued, "but living in a farming community, you must know this is a busy season. Luckily, I have a good deputy I can leave in charge."

"I can see you're just as thoughtful as Hattie told me. I just couldn't believe all the wonderful things she said about how well you treated our little Jesse when she stayed in your town and ah—"

"Belle," Hattie interrupted. "It looks like the plate of buns in the parlor is empty. Would you replace it with this one?"

Once Belle left the room, Jesse spoke. "Russ Martin, you told a bold faced lie on the Sabbath and in front of the good Reverend."

"What did you want me to say?" Russ teased. "Well, Mrs. Clark, I've come here to sweep Jesse off her feet, kidnap her, and take her back to Loveland with me so that I can convince her to be my wife. I must admit it would have given the old biddy something to talk about."

"You certainly have her pegged," Hattie said, not trying to hide her displeasure with the woman.

"There is someone like Belle Clark in every town," Russ said. Turning to Jesse, he continued. "There were people like her in Stillwater, ready to spread all kinds of stories when Ellie died and even more when I left so abruptly to find Clay. There will be another in Loveland as well, ready to spread her vicious gossip about an old sheriff and a young seamstress."

Jesse smiled at Russ. "I think if I can handle this Belle Clark, I can handle just about anyone."

Russ squeezed her hand and led her to the table where two steaming mugs of coffee sat beside a plate of hot cross buns.

"These are delicious, Hattie," Russ said, after savoring his first bite.

"Since you seem to like my cooking, you'll stay for dinner, won't you?" The smile on Hattie's told him she approved of their surprise guest.

"I hadn't given it much thought, but I have no other plans."

David put his hand on Russ' and Jesse's shoulders. "If you two would like some time alone, you can use my buggy."

Jesse left Russ sitting at the table, as she got to her feet and took David aside. "Thank you, Uncle David. We do need some time alone. Russ came here to convince me to return to Loveland and abandon my plans about going to Denver."

"I figured as much. God works in mysterious ways. We weren't happy about you going to Denver alone. Apparently, Gary came to the same conclusion and sent Russ to get you."

"Gary didn't send Russ, not really. He led Russ to believe I'd planned on going directly to Denver without returning to Loveland."

"Why?" David's expression said he couldn't comprehend such a thing.

"I don't know. Maybe he thought it was high time Russ and I found out we cared for each other. Whatever his reasoning, I'm grateful. I'm happier than I've ever been in my life."

"I only worry about his lack of faith," David said, echoing the words she had spoken earlier.

"Don't be. I think God had a little something to do with his decision to come here today. I could almost see a stirring when we were outside. I think God has plans for our friend, Russ Martin."

When they finished eating, they slipped out the back door to the barn. Jesse watched as Russ expertly hitched the horse to the rig.

"Uncle David doesn't like it when I insist on taking the buggy out alone."

"I can understand why," Russ replied, looking down at her cane.

"I'm not an invalid. I can handle a rig. I drove out to the farm alone three weeks ago when I decided to sell it."

"I didn't say you were an invalid. It's just, well, I can understand David's concern. It's not safe for a young lady to be driving alone. Let me worry about you, Jesse." Russ put his hand on her cheek and bent to kiss her lips.

Jesse's knees weakened. As much as she had longed for Russ' touch, she was afraid of her reaction. Would she be repelled, as she'd been with Brian? To her surprise and delight, warmth spread through her body. A contentment, she never thought possible, filled her mind.

Russ held her a moment longer than necessary, giving her a chance to enjoy the feeling. "So," he finally said, "where are you taking me?"

"Out to the farm. I knew I had to go there today to say good-bye to Mama. I'm not too proud to admit I was dreading going out there alone."

Russ held out his hand to help her into the buggy. "The farm it is," he said, as he climbed in beside her and snapped the reins against the back of the horse.

"I haven't ridden a horse since..." Jesse spoke absently, unable to finish what she'd started, unable to understand why she even brought up the subject.

"Say it, Jesse, since you were shot," Russ said.

"I can't. I won't ever be whole again."

Russ put his arm around her shoulders and comforted her. "You've made remarkable progress. You have to give it time."

"I have given it time, Russ."

"Have you? It may seem like it to you, but it's only been six months. It seems longer because you've had nothing else to occupy your mind. Dr. Page told you it would be a long recovery. You must be patient."

Russ drove out of the yard and headed toward the farm before Jesse spoke. "All right, I admit I've been impatient. I promise I'll give it time. Tell me about Gary. Is he truly happy?"

"Back up, Jesse. You're angry about your injury. You have every right to be, so let's talk about it. Don't change the subject to avoid what's on your mind. Talk to me."

"What do you want me to say? How do you want me to feel? Of course, I'm angry. Why shouldn't I be? Caleb took my childhood, and Jeb took my mobility. I'm afraid I'll never walk without this cane. Until today, I've been afraid no one would ever care about me. Do you really care, or do you just feel sorry for me?"

"Feel sorry for you? No, I don't pity you, if that's what you mean. I think I've cared for you ever since the day Clay told me about you."

"Even knowing who my father is?"

"At first I thought it would make a difference, but it doesn't. You're a beautiful frightened young woman. I'm positive Clay told no one other than me about you. I don't know why he trusted me, or why I came to care, but I wouldn't have wanted it any other way. Maybe God touched his heart. Maybe He wanted me to know about you and care for you. Maybe a hundred things, but the one thing I know is you're one part of my life I don't want to lose.

"Believe me, I've tried to stop caring about you. I've told myself a hundred times I shouldn't want to be near you. I should hate you for what Caleb did to Ellie. Instead of believing myself, I've come to care for you more than I should. I want to get to know you, maybe even spend the rest of my life with you, but only if you want the same thing." Again he took her in his arms and kissed her tenderly.

"Oh, Russ, don't ever stop caring about me. I need some time to be me. Help me find the real Jesse Tyler, but please don't stop caring."

Chapter Eleven

The trip from Clarkston to Loveland took over twenty-four hours. Russ and Jesse took the time to talk.

To his surprise, he learned facts about the Tyler gang he never knew before. Jesse voiced her concerns about everything from Gary's feelings toward Russ to the subject of Russ' lack of faith.

He knew his faith had been shaken with Ellie's death, but he also knew something touched him as he sat in the back of the church in Clarkston and listened to Jesse sing. Finding God again might not be as difficult as he originally thought, especially with Jesse to help him find the way.

As for Gary, he found the subject still mystified him. Over the past few months, they formed a truce of sorts, but this game of deception to get him and Jesse together confused him.

As they neared Loveland, Jesse dozed beside him. He worried about her strength. The trip had drained her, and he couldn't help but wonder how she would ever be able to run a business and take care of herself at the same time.

"Jesse," he whispered. "We're pulling into Loveland. See, there's Gary waiting for us."

"Gary?" she murmured, her voice laced with sleep. "You must be mistaken. Gary isn't meeting me. I told him I'd rent a rig. I know he's busy."

She leaned across Russ and peered out the window, to see Gary for herself, standing on the platform. "It is Gary, and Mr. Otto and Clara are with him!"

The train pulled to a stop and Russ got up from his seat, his muscles cramped from the long trip. He waited for Jesse to rise, but made certain he would be the first one off the train. He knew she would need help getting down the step.

Once he alighted from the train, he gently placed his hands around her waist and lifted her from the doorway of the coach. After he put her down, he turned to face Gary. He enjoyed watching the younger man squirm, and beamed at the look of delight on Jesse's face.

"Gary," she said, moving toward him. Exhaustion from the trip showed in her face and forced her to lean heavily on her cane, making her slight limp even more pronounced. "I didn't expect you to meet me."

Gary hugged her tightly. "Am I still in your good graces?" he glanced at Russ, as though the question were meant for both of them.

"Barely," she replied. "Two days ago, I would have gladly had your head. Today, I only want you to have this." She kissed him lightly on the cheek.

"Don't know what Judge Stover would say about the story you told me," Russ said, as he shook Gary's hand. "I trust he won't ever hear of it."

Russ wondered if Gary actually relaxed or if he only imagined it. His deception had been a fool trick, but how could Russ hold it against him? How could he remain angry, when he found Jesse by following his heart?

Clara and Jesse embraced and kissed each other on the cheek, as though they were close friends. "I always wanted a sister," Jesse said. "Russ told me your joyous news, although I guessed as much from Gary's letters."

"I'll take everyone to the cafe for dinner," Eli said. "This young lady looks like she could use a good meal and some rest. Gary, you and Russ collect the baggage while I escort the ladies to the cafe. You can meet us there."

When Eli, Jesse, and Clara crossed the street, Gary turned to Russ. "I hope you don't hate me too much for lyin' to you."

"It was a fool thing to do, and I ought to beat some sense into you for even thinking of it, to say nothing of carrying it out," Russ' spoke sternly. "Do I hate you? I should, but I don't. It if weren't for you, she'd be leaving for Denver."

"Jesse's not goin' to Denver? Is she stayin' here?" Gary looked hopeful.

"Isn't that the reason you wanted me to go to Clarkston?"

"I thought you needed to find out you cared for her. I prayed for her to be as happy as I am. There was something else though. I wanted you to find the Lord the way I have, and I knew Jesse could help."

Russ smiled at him. "I knew I cared for her a long time ago. As for finding the Lord, I think He found me. It wasn't any great revelation, not the way I thought it would be. It came slowly. It will take a while for us to renew our acquaintance, but with Jesse's help I know I can do it. She's changed my life before, I know she can do it again."

"What do you mean she changed your life?"

"When Caleb killed Ellie, I wanted only revenge. I thought I'd find what I wanted in Slack Creek. Then for some unknown reason, Clay wanted to talk to me, wanted to bear his soul. When he told me about Jesse, I couldn't believe it. Since I never read anything about her I thought he told me a convincing story. Last fall, when I met her, I realized his words didn't do her justice. I wanted to protect her. I still do. When you came to her rescue, I was afraid you wanted to finish what Jeb started.

"On Sunday, I listened as she sang and warmth filled my heart. I need time to think about what happened, but I think God used her voice to open my heart. I know you and I have been at odds since the first day and with good cause, but for Jesse's sake, I'd like to start over and try to be friends."

"Then the two of you will be gettin' married?"

"Not for a while. Don't rush things. Jesse needs some time."

"Time? Time for what?"

"Time to be Jesse. Time to realize there is a whole world out there. Time to see if she has feelings for me. She said I could court her, but I want her to be sure before we get married."

"I guess it's a start," Gary replied, his eyebrows knotted. "Is she strong enough?"

"What do you mean?" Russ stared at him.

"When she got off the train, I couldn't believe what I saw. I expected her to look like … like Jesse. Instead, she looked so tired."

"The trip exhausted her," Russ said, as he located Jesse's bags and paid a young man to take them to his office.

"The trip exhausted her?" Gary turned Russ' statement into a question. "How could a train trip of little more than a day exhaust her? She's used to riding for days on end when we would go into Mexico for the winter, and return again in the spring, to say nothing of when we were being chased by a posse."

"The excitement and anticipation took their toll. Face it Gary, the Longs sheltered her. She did little but sit and sew. Sure, David insisted she use the crutches and learn to walk again, but she did precious little else. I don't understand how she ever thought she could start a new life in Denver."

Gary nodded. "It's been bothering me, too. Why a dress shop? I know she's good with a needle. She sewed for us as well as the Mendozas, but why would she want to do it for a living?"

"What else is she suited for? She can shoot a gun, attend to five men, and dig out bullets. Those aren't particularly good qualifications for any kind of job for a respectable young lady. She's not the schoolteacher type and she's not suited to be a dance hall girl either. She'll do just fine. I've looked into a little house down the street. It should be perfect for her. I asked the banker to start getting the papers ready before I left for Clarkston."

"You must have been pretty sure that you could persuade her to stay."

"Not sure at all, just hopeful. It seems as though everything is going to work out the way we both want it."

* * * *

At the cafe, Jesse recognized Gary's concern about her appearance had increased, rather than dissipated.

"You'll spend a few days with us at the farm, won't you?" he said.

"Of course, she will," Eli interrupted, not giving Jesse a chance to decline.

"I have things to do in town," Jesse protested.

"A week of rest won't hurt you, Jes," Gary said, patting her hand.

She withdrew it, as though Gary's touch burned like a hot poker. "Don't you understand, Gary, I've had six months of rest. I want to work. I have to do something. I want to put everything behind me and start new."

"It will take a good week to get the house ready for you," Russ said. "By then, you'll be rested and ready to start."

"You're as bad as Gary. What do you think you're doing, patting me on the head, and telling me to be a good little girl? Well, I'm not a good little girl. I want to see the house right now. I want to be the one to get it ready to move into."

Gary threw up his hands in disgust. "Never could argue with you, but as long as we're here in town, you will let Dr. Page check you over."

"There's no need. Dr. Page has enough to keep him busy without me. It looks like he's even taken you on as a patient."

She knew her statement would upset her brother. She'd thrown in the part about him to take his mind off her stubbornness. She'd noticed his new spectacles earlier, but said nothing. Now, in her anger, she groped at any weapon she could find.

"If you mean the spectacles, yes, he did insist on them. For the first time, I can see straight. I can see you're exhausted."

Jesse tired of the argument, of seeing Gary so upset over her. "All right, this once I'll let you win. I'll see Dr. Page, I'll do ... well, I'll see Dr. Page."

Gary smiled. "I liked it better when you were about to say you'd do as you were told."

"I'm sick and tired of doing what everyone tells me," she snapped.

"It's for your own good, Jesse," Russ said, his voice filled with concern. "I told you to let me worry about you for a while."

"I ain't used to it, I mean I'm not used to it," she corrected herself.

"Sounds like Aunt Hattie's been improvin' your talkin'," Gary teased.

"Yes, she has. I intend to be a lady, a well-respected lady. I'll make it happen, too, just as soon as I get rid of this...this cane."

Chapter Twelve

Loveland, Missouri, March, 1890

"Do you know what tomorrow signifies, Jesse?" Russ said. He put down the towel he was using to dry the dishes he'd insisted on helping her wash up before going back to the jail.

"Since tomorrow is Easter," she replied. "You must be thinking it's been a year since you brought me back where I belong. You know last year Easter came in April and this year it's much earlier."

Jesse's comment made Russ break into a wide grin. "There's something I've been wanting to tell you. I've thought about keeping it a secret until tomorrow, but I want you to know it now."

"What is it, Russ?"

"I've been meeting with Rev. Terrill on a regular basis. Tomorrow, I'm going to profess my faith and join the church."

Jesse could hardly believe her ears. She had prayed for this to happen ever since they returned to Loveland. At first Russ seemed reluctant to go to church with her, but he made the effort. She had been able to see his faith building, but wondered if he could feel it in his heart. It came so slowly, she wondered if she imagined it. She'd often asked herself what she expected. It certainly wasn't the slow building she witnessed. Did she expect God to strike Russ blind, as he had Saul on the road to Damascus? She smiled at the thought of Russ being helpless and blind. Although it had not been so dramatic, she knew the slow building of faith was best. It gave her a chance to get to know Russ better and examine her feelings for him.

"Are you all right, Jesse?" Russ took her hand in his before he pressed it to his lips.

"Yes, I'm very all right. I'm overwhelmed is more like it. You don't know how long and hard I've prayed for you to find the Lord. I know it hasn't been easy for you. Considering the suffering you've endured at the hands of Caleb Tyler, it's been a long hard road."

She began to cry, and Russ wiped away the tears from her cheeks with his thumb. His calluses were rough, but his touch remained gentle.

"Don't cry, Jesse. I love you too much to ever want you to be sad."

"Oh, Russ, these aren't tears of sadness. They're tears of joy. I've been so afraid to admit my feelings for you. Until you could accept the Lord, I knew I could never accept you. For the first time in a year, I can consider the future."

"I want you in my future, Jesse. I can't wait any longer. Will you marry me?

Russ' question took her by surprise and yet it was one she had been expecting. Now, she could say yes without a moment of hesitation.

"I'd be proud to be your wife," she whispered before allowing him to take her in his arms and kiss her lovingly.

* * * *

Jesse sat at her sewing table. A light breeze rustled the curtains in the shop. She'd just finished Julia Page's final fitting for her wedding dress and now made notes on the alternation necessary to complete the project.

She should be working on her own wedding dress. She remembered Saturday evening when she and Russ sat in her kitchen eating supper. She'd been so comfortable with him sitting at her table. His proposal had been the one thing she wanted to hear. With her acceptance, she could now think of having a real life, one that included Russ as her husband.

She smiled to herself remembering her joy at saying yes. The long evening of loving kisses and caresses that followed wrapped her in love. Now all she had to do was set the date, and she would become Mrs. Russell Martin. Once that happened, Jesse Tyler would cease to exist.

She'd been trying, day by day, to walk a little further without the cane. It wouldn't be long before she would be rid of it. Dr. Page seemed impressed with her progress.

So much had happened. It sometimes seemed all too much to comprehend. Gary and Clara had been married just before Christmas. She'd stood beside Clara, while Russ stood with Gary, and she'd envied them.

Just last week, they announced their first baby would be coming in the fall. The announcement prompted Jesse to search her fabrics for just the right pieces for a layette.

The shop, surprisingly, had prospered, until now she had so many customers she'd begun contemplating hiring someone to help.

Voices drifted in on the breeze. Men's voices, which were painfully familiar. Looking up from her work, she saw her father, Frank, and Ruben dismounting their horses. There would be no time for her to hide. Her cane lay too far away for her to retrieve it and lock the door before they could entered.

Quickly she opened the drawer of her sewing table. Her fingers caressed the smooth pearl handle of the Colt. Russ disliked her having it in the shop, and she'd promised him weeks ago, she would get rid of it. Thank goodness she hadn't done so.

The bell above the door jingled merrily as Caleb entered the shop. "Why Jesse Girl, Jesse Girl, we thought we'd lost you for good. Then a man came and told us you were alive. I rejoiced. I rejoiced in the Lord."

"Don't, Pa. Piety doesn't become you," Jesse replied, coldly.

"I did, Jesse Girl, I rejoiced. I told your bother we must go and find that prodigal child and bring her home."

"I am home, Pa. You have no home, unless you're talking about the bordello you're so fond of. How much is she going to pay you for me, two hundred, three hundred, more?"

"Where is your brother, Jesse Girl?" Caleb shouted, in what she knew was an attempt to stop her accusations.

Jesse panicked. She couldn't endanger Gary. He had too much to live for. For her, it didn't matter. She had no child on the way, no husband.

Perhaps it had been best she and Russ hadn't set a date as yet and had waited a year before agreeing to marry. At least Russ wouldn't have to suffer at the hands of her father for a second time. She only had herself to consider.

"They hanged him," she declared, trying to sound convincing.

"You're lyin' to me, Jesse Girl."

"They did," she pleaded. "Gary came to find me, and they arrested him. They held a trial. They found him guilty, guilty as you. Wasn't that what you wanted?"

Caleb's eyes were cold. "You wouldn't have stayed here if they'd hanged him."

"Where else did I have to go?" She forced tears to flow.

"You had the farm and your ma's sister and her preacher husband."

"There is no farm. Ma asked Hattie to sell it. As for Hattie and David, they have their own lives to live. They didn't want to be saddled with me again. At least here there were people who cared, people who had been good to me."

"So we heard," Frank said. "We heard about a certain sheriff who cares."

Jesse's mind spun. How could they know about Russ? "You're wrong," she protested.

"You were seen, Jesse Girl," Caleb accused. "You can't deny it. You were seen all cozied up with that sheriff."

"He was being polite," Jesse countered.

"How often is he polite, Jes?" Frank said. "Is he polite in bed? Does he say please and thank you?"

"You have a filthy mind. I never let Ruben and Jeb touch me, and no one else has either."

"That's what I wanted to hear, Jesse Girl," Caleb said, his rotted teeth and fetid breath sickening her.

"Where's Jeb?" she said, hoping if she changed the subject, she could catch them off guard long enough to pull her gun. "Is he sneaking in through the back to shoot me like he did before?"

"Not this time, Jesse Girl. Jeb is dead."

"Now you're the one who is lying, Pa,"

"Not this time. I killed him because he couldn't complete a job. He told us you were dead, and you're not. He lied to me. Now, I ask you again, where's your brother?"

"I told you, he's dead," she screamed.

Caleb moved closer to her and Jesse stood, supporting herself against the table. Once she awkwardly got to her feet, she pulled the gun from the drawer.

"Don't come any closer, Pa," she said, her voice so calm it frightened her.

"You wouldn't kill me, Jesse Girl. What about them words you live by, 'honor thy father and thy mother'?"

"My mother is dead, and I don't have a father. He died the first time he walked out of my life."

"Why, Jesse Girl, I'm your father, you know that," Caleb sneered.

"You're a rutting old goat!"

Caleb took another step, as Jesse deliberately pulled the trigger. The look on his face, the shock, and disbelief, scared her. She'd become what he wanted her to become, a ruthless killer, like Frank.

Before she knew it, Frank seized the opportunity of catching her off guard. Grabbing her hand, he pointed the gun harmlessly toward the ceiling as it discharged for a second time. With a quick twist of her wrist, he made Jesse drop the gun. Something snapped, like a dry twig and the pain became instantly intense. No matter how painful it felt, she refused to let him see how she'd been hurt.

Frank slapped her hard, so hard, she reeled backwards, hitting her head against a second table that stood behind her.

"You shot, Pa!" Frank shouted, forcing her to remain conscious.

Clumsily, she stood back up, her head throbbing, and the room in front of her spinning. "I shot a rabid animal. I put it out of its misery," she shouted back.

He grabbed her again and slapped her. "You're comin' with us. Don't think I won't hesitate to kill you!"

Jesse laughed at the stupidity of Frank's statement. "You won't kill me, Frank. I'm worth too much money to you. I know what Pa planned to do with me in Mexico. He would have taken me back down there and given me to Isabella. She would have paid good money for me."

"How did you know about it?"

"I talked to Gary before they hanged him. He told me," she said, trying to remain calm.

"He couldn't have known. Pa just told me a few days ago," Frank said, tightening his grip on her wrist. "It don't matter none. You're comin' with us."

"What about Caleb? Are you just going to leave him here? He isn't dead you know. I didn't shoot him bad enough to kill him."

"He's dead, or as good as," Frank snapped. "You know yourself, if it were you or me, he wouldn't hesitate to leave us. Now come on. Get her gun, Ruben."

"My cane," Jesse insisted. "I need my cane."

Ruben bent to pick it up. "Leave it there," Frank barked. "We'll just throw her on Pa's horse. She won't be doin' no walkin' where she's goin'."

* * * *

Russ turned back to the stack of papers on his desk. His visit with Gary had delayed the work he had to do. Gary and Eli had brought Clara into town to see Dr. Page and stopped by to visit, while they waited for her.

Before Russ could become completely engrossed in the work hat hand, Gary returned to the office. "Give me a gun, Russ," he demanded, as he entered.

"You know I can't."

"Give him the gun," Eli said. "While you're at it, give me one, too."

"What's going on?" Russ demanded, as he unlocked the case where the rifles were stored.

"Caleb and Frank just went into Jesse's place. They have Ruben with them," Gary said.

Without hesitation, Russ tossed Gary a rifle and handed one to Eli as well. "I'll take the front. You and Eli go in through the kitchen."

They'd just started down the street, when a shot rang out and Russ' heart sank. Had Caleb finished what Jeb started? Moments later, a second shot followed.

He hurried down the street toward the front of the shop, as Gary and Eli went around to the back of the house and slipped in through the kitchen.

Why had he insisted she get rid of her gun, her only means of protection? He hated the questions his mind posed as he rounded the corner. He ran toward the front of the shop, his heart pounding. Frank and Ruben were just leaving, pushing Jesse in front of them.

Jesse's face and dress were splattered with blood, but whose blood? Strands of hair had come loose from her neat bun. Her face was drained of color, except for where a bruise had begun to appear around the cut on her lip. She looked dazed.

"Hold it right there, Frank," Russ ordered, as he raised his rifle.

"I'll kill her, Lawman," Frank spat. "Put down the gun or I swear I'll kill her."

"He won't kill me, Russ," Jesse said, her voice sounding weak. "I'm worth too much money to him in Mexico. Let him take me, just let him take me. I'm the one they want. They know you hanged Gary."

Russ cringed at her lie, but tried not to show it.

"Put your gun down, Russ," she pleaded, when he said nothing. "I'm not worth losing your life over."

"She makes good sense, Lawman. What was it she called you, Russ?" Frank sneered. "Are you special to her, Russ?"

"Just a friend," he lied.

"Tylers don't have lawmen for friends. Ain't no one ever told you that?"

"I'm taking you in, Frank," Russ retorted, not lowering his gun.

"You got the wrong Tyler, Lawman," Frank continued. "You want Jesse. She just killed Pa. She ain't no better than the rest of us. She's a murderer."

"NO," Jesse cried, tears washing the blood from her face. "I gave him warning. He wouldn't stop."

Russ watched as the impact of Frank's words hit Jesse like a slap in the face.

"I warned him Russ. I warned him, and he wouldn't stop."

"You killed him, Jes!" Frank shouted above her words, his mouth close to her ear. "You broke one of them Commandments you used to throw in my face. 'Thou shalt not kill.' Ain't that what you used to tell me?"

Russ saw Gary and Eli in the doorway and breathed a sigh of relief.

"Let her go, Frank," Gray said, the barrel of his gun pushing into Frank's back. "I may not be a crack shot, like Jes, but at this range, I can't miss."

"You're dead, Gary," Frank said. "Jes said you were hanged." Frank turned his head back to Jesse and again shouted in her ear. "Pa said you were lyin, Jes, but I thought not Jes. Jes wouldn't lie. Don't that God of yours say something about lyin? Ain't it some kind of a sin?"

"Let her go, Frank," Gary repeated. "Let her go and drop the gun."

Frank dropped his revolver to the ground, and shoved Jesse as he released her.

Rushing up the steps, Russ then pulled Jesse's Colt from Ruben's belt. As he led his prisoners away, he shot her a glance he hoped said he was glad she hadn't done what he'd told her to do.

With the drama over, a crowd began to gather, including Dr. Page and Brian McPhearson. Clara stood on the edge of the turmoil and elbowed her way to the front.

"Caleb's been shot, Doc," Gary said. "He's in the shop. Keep Jes out of there."

Russ glanced back toward where Jesse lay. He wanted to go to her, but he had other duties to attend. As soon as he could, he could come back and comfort her.

Jesse lay on the ground, her sobs hardly audible. "We'll take care of everything," Brian said, kneeling beside her.

She tried to protest, but Brian wouldn't listen. Effortlessly, he picked her up to carry her into the house. When he first touched her, she began to whimper like a hurt puppy.

"It's all right, Jesse. It's over," he whispered.

"Don't touch me," she cried.

Brian again ignored her plea. Without further comment, he carried her into the house and put her to bed.

Jesse let everything wash over her. She didn't want to open her eyes, didn't want to see Caleb lying in his own blood on her floor.

"I think Jesse will be more comfortable if you leave, Brian," Jesse heard Clara say. "Dr. Page may need your help. Before you go, please bring me a basin of water."

How many other people would invade her house? Why couldn't they just leave her alone?

"Can I help?" Brenna spoke as she entered the room.

"Thank you, Brenna," Clara replied. "She has a bad cut on the back of her head and look at her wrist."

"What did they do to you?" Brenna said.

"They made me one of them," she whispered, breaking her resolve to remain silent. "They made me one of them," she repeated louder, the tone of her voice bordering on hysteria. "Russ will have no recourse but to arrest me. I shot my father."

"Ssh," Brenna crooned consolingly. "We're going to take care of you. Everything will be all right."

Gently, Brenna washed the blood and tears from Jesse's face, making her to cringe when the cloth touched her bruised cheek.

"Who hit you?"

"Frank."

"And the cut on the back of your head," Brenna pressed.

"I don't know. Maybe it happened when I fell," she replied flatly. "Is Caleb dead?"

"I don't know. I haven't been in there."

"It's over, isn't it?" Jesse questioned.

Brenna smiled. "Yes, it's over. You don't have to be afraid of them anymore."

"That's not what I meant. My life here is over, isn't it?"

"Of course not," Brenna said, reassuringly. "You rest. Russ will be anxious to see you."

* * * *

Russ wished he could be at Jesse's side. From the expression on Gary's face, he knew Gary wanted to be there as well. Unfortunately, they had no alternative. Russ had already begun deputizing several men for an around the clock guard, but in his heart knew it would not be necessary. The Tyler gang no longer existed. The chances of anyone trying to break them out of jail were slim to none.

"Where's Jeb?" Russ heard Gary ask, when the men he'd once ridden with were locked in their cells.

"He's dead," Frank replied, his voice less menacing than it had been earlier. "When Pa found out Jes was alive, he killed Jeb. He just pulled out his gun and shot him like he would a rattler."

Russ began to listen more intently, began to watch not only Gary's reaction to Frank, but Frank's reaction to Gary.

Frank put his face close to the bars of the cell and, looking into Gary's eyes, continued. "I don't understand why they ain't got Jes in this cell? That was a fool trick she played, pullin' a gun. For that matter, why are you runnin' free?"

"I ain't free, Frank. At least not yet. I stood trial. They found me guilty of the bank robberies, but not of murder. I go nowhere without checking with Russ first. As for Jes, she never had been wanted, except for what Pa was planning. He wanted her for that bordello Isabella runs, didn't he?"

"It's where she belonged. As for you, free or not, you should still be with Pa."

"Jes wouldn't have survived a week in that place. I thank God everyday for allowing both of us to get away from Pa. Here I have a life. I've got a wife and a baby on the way. Jes has a life here too, a life with Russ."

"So, it's true. She's truckin' with a lawman."

Russ hated the sound of Frank's voice, the accusations, but he didn't interfere. Gary could handle the situation. For the first time in his life, Gary had the upper hand over Frank.

"Russ and Jes are going to be married."

Frank laughed loudly. "Don't count on it. Jes knows no lawman would be content married to a lyin', murderin' Tyler."

"Jes ain't no murderer," Gary snapped.

"What do you call what she did to Pa?

"Fear, self defense, not murder," Russ replied, involving himself in the conversation for the first time.

"I don't recall talkin' to you, lawman," Frank said. "This is between Gary and me."

Returning his attention to Gary, Frank continued. "Did Jes turn you into one of those Bible spouters, Gary?"

"No, the love of God turned me around. I go to church. I believe, if that's what you mean."

"Did Hattie really sell the farm?"

"Jes sold it."

"Then she did have a place to go other than here. She's a good liar.

Pa said she was lyin'."

"Did you ever think she might have been trying to get you to leave her alone?"

"Not for a minute. She lied to save you. You were always good at hidin' behind a woman's skirts, first Ma's and now Jesse's. Too bad we ain't takin' her to Mexico. I could have held out for a thousand instead of the five hundred Isabella promised Pa. There's just one thing I want to know. How did you figure out what Pa intended to do?"

"Consuela told me."

"Consuela? The little wench," Frank spat. "The night you had her, it had to have been when she told you. Pa didn't pay her for nothin' but spreadin' her legs."

Russ watched, as Gary smiled for the first time. "I didn't have her, Frank. I didn't want her. She understood me, more than you or Caleb or anyone ever understood me."

* * * *

Jesse lay on the bed, tears washing her cheeks. Dr. Page had taken care of the cut on her head and set her broken wrist. Brenna and Clara had washed the cuts and bruises on her face. One eye was swollen shut and she could feel the tenderness of the bruises. When she licked her dry lips, she found them swollen as well.

"Can I see her?" She heard Russ say.

She forced herself to listen as Clara told Russ what she said earlier. "She doesn't want to see anyone."

"She can't mean it," he pleaded.

"She doesn't want to see you," Clara protested.

"I'll go in first," Gary said.

"She doesn't want to see you either," Clara declared.

"Well, she's going to see me," Gary shouted, just before she heard him enter the room.

"Jes, Russ wants—"

"Go away Gary," she interrupted. "Didn't Clara tell you I don't want to see you?"

"She told me, but I won't go away. Russ is here, too."

"I definitely don't want to see Russ. It's over, Gary."

"What did they do to you? Talk to me. I know you love Russ. Why are you shutting him out?"

"Love?" Jesse said, the word slurred through her swollen lips. "I don't know the meaning of the word love, Gary. I'm a Tyler, and you know what it means to be a Tyler."

"You're not one of them, Jes."

"I shot my father. Did I kill him? Nobody will tell me."

"You didn't kill him. He'll live long enough to hang."

"They've taken everything from me," Jesse continued, tears flowing freely. "I have nothing left."

"You're wrong. You have Russ."

"I don't have Russ. I don't even have God anymore. It's all gone."

"Russ wants to see you."

"No! I can't stand to see him."

"Clara and I will stay here tonight. By morning you'll feel differently."

"No one will stay tonight. I want to be alone. I don't want you here, now or ever. Can't you understand?"

"No, I can't," Gary replied, taking her in his arms and holding her while she sobbed.

"We'll leave, if that's what you want, but we'll come back."

* * * *

Russ paced nervously, waiting for Gary to reenter the room. "I tried, I really tried," Gary said, shaking his head.

"I'm going in there and make her talk to me," Russ insisted.

"She just fell asleep. Give her until morning."

Chapter Thirteen

Jesse awoke early. She knew if she didn't get up now, Russ would come to the house before she was ready for him. She could still see the hurt in his eyes, the condemnation when he'd removed her gun from Ruben's belt. She could hear him insisting she get rid of it. She knew she could never live with what she'd done, not and still be Jesse Tyler and not and still love Russ.

"Why God?" she pleaded. "Why couldn't You let me be happy? Maybe Caleb was right after all. Maybe You don't care what happens to the likes of me. If You did, You would have kept Pa from finding me. You would have let me be happy. I've been a fool to think You existed. I'm the only one who can take charge of my life. I should have gone to Denver the way I planned. Maybe then none of this would have happened."

By the time Russ arrived, the doors were locked and the shades drawn.

"Jesse," she heard him call, when his knock went unanswered. "Jesse, let me in."

"No, Russ. I can't."

"Please, Jesse, let me in."

"You heard me. I said no, Russ. I thought I made it clear to Gary last night. I don't want to see you."

She held back her tears. There would be plenty of time for them later. For now, she wouldn't let him know he'd made her cry, wouldn't let him know how it hurt to send him away.

Eventually, he left, but he kept coming back, kept begging to see her.

Any chores she had to do outside, were done late at night, when there was no one around. Her mirror showed her a distorted face—a grotesque image of herself.

She worked, ignoring the dizziness and the pain, cleaning the house and writing a farewell note to Russ.

Finally, she packed her saddlebags, taking as little of her life with her as possible. She took only a change of riding clothes, a few tins of food, and the tin plate picture of Russ. She lovingly touched the picture and remembered how they had them taken at the county fair last summer. Russ had the matching picture of her.

From beneath the floorboards of the kitchen, she retrieved the money she'd put there. The years of riding with her father had destroyed her trust in banks.

She cried, as she remembered scrubbing the blood from the floor of the shop. Her head and body ached as again and again she relived the nightmare of Frank's final beating.

When, at last, she finished all she needed to do, she read over the letter to Russ. Her broken right wrist forced her to print the words with her left hand, making it look more like a letter from a small child than a grown woman.

> My dear, dear Russ,
>
> I do love you. Right now, I'm certain you find it hard to believe. I can't stay here, and I can't have the one thing I want the most, you. No lawman should be saddled with a Tyler, and I am a Tyler. I'm as bad as Caleb and Frank and the others. I hope they hang.
>
> I'm glad Pa will die by someone's hand other than mine At least I don't think he's dead, unless, of course, Gary lied to me.
>
> I've broken too many commandments to stay here. Too many to even believe God exists any more. I've lied and tried to take a man's life.
>
> I have to put things in order. I must have been a fool to think Jesse Tyler could have a life.
>
> Don't try to find me, Russ. It won't be worth the effort.
>
> I love you,

Jesse

When she finished reading the letter, she sat for a moment and wondered how it would feel to be called by a name other than Jesse Tyler and to live somewhere other than Loveland.

As usual, she heard Russ pounding on her door in the morning. "Jesse, Jesse, open this door," he demanded, his voice filled with exasperation.

"No, Russ," she said.

"I have to talk to you. The trial is tomorrow. I need you, Jesse."

"You have Gary."

"Open this door!"

She left his plea unanswered and waited until she heard him leave her porch. Assured he was walking away from her house, she pulled aside the shade and looked out the window in the hopes of catching a glimpse of him. As she did, he turned, and she saw him, momentarily, for perhaps the last time.

Late that night, she placed the note on the table, raised the shade, unlocked the door, and left the house, as well as Russ, behind.

The years of riding with her father had given her the endurance she needed to ride through the night and well into the next day. She drew on her memory of what happened in Loveland to gain the strength to put her pain as well as her exhaustion to the back of her mind. She became oblivious to everything but her need to put the past behind her.

She headed toward New Orleans. She knew Russ would never look for her there. She didn't stop until she'd ridden well into Louisiana.

* * * *

Russ didn't go to Jesse's house in the morning. There were too many things going on with the trial and all the extra people in town. He hoped Gary would persuade her to come. The days of being at his office with Caleb and Frank in the cell made him ache to see her, to hold her in his arms and wipe away the hurt her father and brother had inflicted on her. He'd only seen her, momentarily, the morning before when she pulled aside the shade. The look in her eyes tormented him ever since. Had he been wrong to abide by her wishes? Perhaps it would have been better if he kicked in her door and forced her to talk to him.

At last Gary and Clara arrived. When Clara had been seated, Gary made his way to Russ' side, his expression grave.

"She's not coming, is she?" Russ said, hoping Gary's answer would prove him wrong.

"She's gone, Russ," Gary replied, his voice low, his tone one of despair.

"Should it surprise me?"

"I don't know. I never thought she'd do anything like this, not just leave without a word."

"Why not?" Russ said, his tone cold. "It's exactly what she planned to do when you sent me to bring her back from Clarkston. She'd planned to go to Denver, start a new life with a new name, and disappear."

"She left you a note." Gary handed Russ an envelope, his name painstakingly printed in a childish scrawl.

"I can't read it now," Russ said, shoving the envelope into the pocket of his vest. "When this is over—"

"I understand," Gary interrupted, "but you are going to find her, aren't you? She loves you."

"Does she?" Russ answered Gary's question with one of his own. "Should I chase the wind? If she wants to disappear, how do you expect me to find her?"

"I just thought—"

"You always did have a problem with thinkin', Gary," Frank said, joining the conversation uninvited. "You should never try to think. You ain't got the mind for it. If you hadn't thought, hadn't made a fuss, Jes would have done as we said. Will and Clay wouldn't have died in that mess in Slack Creek."

"Shut up, Frank. This is between me and Russ."

"You and Jes, both of you think you're so much better than Pa and me. Well, let me tell you, neither of you are as innocent as you think you are. You'll burn in Hell, just like the rest of us, especially Jes. She's a Tyler, no matter what she thinks. She proved it when she shot Pa. You didn't see the look in her eyes when she pulled the trigger. They were cold, just like Pa's eyes when he shot the stranger who told him where to find her. She's had her taste of blood and believe me, a taste is never enough."

Frank's words were still burning in Russ' mind when he stood at the front of the courtroom. "All rise. This court is now in session. The Honorable Judge Stovar presiding."

The trial ended almost before it began. The verdict was pronounced less than ten minutes after the jury left to deliberate the fate of the three men before them.

"We find the defendants, Caleb Tyler, Frank Tyler, and Ruben Morris guilty on all counts."

Judge Stovar faced the three men. "Two years ago, I had a young man before me by the name of Tyler. I listened to the testimony he and his sister gave, and I prayed I'd never have to sit in judgment of their father and brother. Today you both stand before me, and I've been, again, sickened by your actions. You've been found guilty of bank robbery and murder, many times over. I hereby sentence you to death, by hanging. The sentence is to be carried out at noon tomorrow, and may God have mercy on your souls."

The crowd in the packed room cheered, as Russ' deputies escorted the men back to the jail. Russ remained behind, not wanting to even be close to these men, these animals, who'd stolen away the only two people he'd ever truly loved in his life. He wished the hanging would be held today and not tomorrow. He wanted a lynch mob to appear in the street tonight, but he knew it wouldn't happen. Tomorrow, tomorrow would see the end of the Tyler gang, or would it?

Had Frank been right? Once Jesse tasted blood, would she ever be the same, or would she crave to kill again, as had her brothers and father?

Russ hadn't seen Levi Abbot in the courtroom earlier. Perhaps he hadn't wanted to see him. Now Levi stood in front of him.

"It's finally over," Levi said. "This time you do have Ellie's killers, and they're going to pay for what they did to you."

"Are they? I don't think hanging will ever cause them the pain they've caused me. For them, it will be over quickly. I'll live with it for the rest of my life."

Levi looked stunned at his answer, but managed to compose himself. "What about the young man and his sister, Gary and Jesse? How are they handling this?"

"You saw Gary sitting in the courtroom today and heard his testimony. What do you think?"

"I'm pleased we asked for mercy two years ago, but I didn't see his sister. The rumor, around town, is she's the one who shot Caleb. I thought she'd surely be here to see justice done."

Russ turned on his old friend. "Well, she isn't. She left town. Maybe everyone was right when they said she'd turn out like the rest of them." Russ turned and left Levi to stare after him.

* * * *

Russ saw Gary standing with the crowd that had gathered to witness the hangings. He wondered what thoughts were running through Gary's mind as the three men were brought from the jail to meet their destiny.

Caleb, hard cold Caleb, cringed at the hangman's noose. Frank had cried at the sight of the three ropes tied side by side. Ruben had to be forcibly carried up the steps to the gallows, fighting his captors all the way, like a wild animal. One by one the ropes were put around their necks and hoods placed over their heads.

Frank's last words came as almost a ghostly sound. "I'll see you in Hell, Gary. Mark my words, I'll be waiting for you and Jesse."

Russ experienced a cold dread as Reverend Wallace read the words of comfort while the three men waited for the trap door to open and their lives come to a dramatic end. The thud of the door giving way and then the snap of the ropes as they grew taut and broke their necks Russ would carry in his heart for the rest of his life. These men were outlaws, killers, but they were also Jesse's father and her oldest brother. Of the Tyler gang, the Tyler family, only Gary and Jesse were left and now even she'd run away. He wondered if Gary experienced the same despair as he did.

Russ turned from the grizzly scene to see if he could find Gary. To his surprise, he saw the young man walking away. Others could take care of the bodies and clean up the mess, he needed to talk to Gary, to try to find out where Jesse might have gone.

"I thought I saw you heading here," Russ said, as he entered the small garden behind Jesse's house. "I read Jesse's letter. You were right.

103

I have to find her. I love her too much to lose her. Do you have any idea where she went?"

Gary looked up, as though trying to comprehend the words. He remained silent for a moment. "She could have gone back to the canyon, but I doubt it. I honestly don't know where you could even begin to look for her. She could be anywhere, Denver, Mexico, Kansas City. It's a big country, Russ, and she has a two day head start."

Chapter Fourteen

Madam DuPre ran the boarding house along the Mississippi River not all that far from Loveland. This was where Jesse finally ended her frightened flight. Calling herself Kate Cross, she explained how she ran away from an abusive husband and needed the woman's protection.

Jesse liked the Creole lady and regretted the lie she'd told. Madam DuPre had been anxious to help Jesse fashion a new wardrobe and purchase a traveling case. She also found a buyer for the gray and the Winchester.

When she questioned the cane, Jesse told her she'd been injured as a child in a riding accident.

After a month, Jesse found her strength returned sufficiently to leave for New Orleans. Once she boarded the train she lay Kate Cross, like Jesse Tyler, to rest.

On the short ride to New Orleans, she became Laurel Morgan. Laurel came from Illinois. Her mother had died several years ago, and her father and brother were killed in a tragic accident just months prior to her departure for Louisiana. After selling the family farm, she'd traveled to New Orleans, where she visited her aunt, Lizette DuPre. Now, the time had come to continue with her life. With the remainder of her inheritance she would be moving west.

Jesse booked passage to Dubuque, and, once in her cabin, counted her money. If she spent it carefully, there would be enough to see her through until she could get to Denver.

On the first night out, she visited the salon after dinner. Selecting a secluded table, she sat alone and listened to the piano player. She softly sang the words to the songs the man played and watched the tables where men and women played poker. Having learned the game from her father and brothers, she knew her expertise at it, no matter what variation the dealer chose, would surpass the other players.

Across the room, she saw a distinguished man watching her intently. He looked to be a bit older than Russ, yet younger than Caleb. Unable to take her eyes from him, almost afraid he would try to talk to her, she watched as he took a match from the pocket of his vest. With one swift movement, he struck the head of the match against the sole of his boot and lit the long, thin cigar, he'd produced from the same pocket. With cigar in hand, he made his way to her table.

"Good evening," he greeted her. "Allow me to introduce myself. My name is Jason Bellinger. Do you mind if I join you?"

Although his question frightened her, she knew she had no reason to distrust him. "It would be a pleasure, Mr. Bellinger."

"Why thank you, Miss..."

"Morgan," Jesse lied. "Laurel Morgan."

"I couldn't help but overhear you singing along with the piano. You have a beautiful voice."

Her cheeks redden at his comment. "I didn't realize anyone could hear me. It seems a shame they don't have a singer, but then I suppose it would distract from the card games."

"You seem very interested in the gaming, Miss Morgan. Do you play cards?"

"I've been known to play a spirited game of whist at home, but this game seems quite interesting."

"Would you like to play a hand or two?" Jason said.

"I wouldn't know how."

Jason dropped the subject. Instead, he asked about her reason for traveling alone. As she had practiced to herself ever since leaving Madam DuPre, she proceeded to tell him the incredible story about her life in Illinois and the recent loss of her father and brother.

When he offered her a drink, she declined, but ordered a mint tea instead. "Oh look," she said, anxious to change the subject. "The piano player is coming back."

"Would you care to sing with him?" Jason prompted.

"I don't know. I'm afraid I'm much too shy to sing for a group of strangers, but it would be fun."

"Perhaps I can arrange something for tomorrow evening, as a lark so to say. It would give you a fond remembrance of your trip north."

For the rest of the trip, Jason became her constant companion. He persuaded her to sing in the salon, and she smiled as he taught her to play black jack and poker.

"Where will you go from here, Laurel?" Jason said, on the night before the boat was scheduled to dock in Dubuque.

"I honestly don't know," she replied, realizing this was the first truly honest answer she had given him since they met.

"Would you consider coming with me to Virginia City?"

His suggestion took her by surprise. She trusted this man and now he turned out to be no better than Caleb. He only wanted her to grace an upstairs bedroom and bestow her favors on any man who had the money to pay for her time.

"Don't misunderstand me, Laurel," he hastily continued. "I went to New Orleans to engage a singer for my gaming club, The Mother Lode. I'm afraid I'm returning empty handed. After hearing you sing and seeing how quickly you learned to play cards, I would like to hire you for the position."

"Why Mr. Bellinger, it sounds as though you're proposing something I'm unprepared to accept."

"Not at all. You would be well paid and have a room of your own. Of course, I would never expect a lady of your stature to entertain my guests privately, if you understand my meaning."

She thought for only a moment before accepting the offer. Virginia City would be as far away from Caleb Tyler's territory as she could hope to get. Jason's offer would give her a new life, a fresh start.

"Are you certain I wouldn't have to..." She couldn't find the strength to say the words. The memory of Frank and his plans, as well as those of her father, burned in her mind.

"I give you my word. You will be respected and cherished by everyone in Virginia City, and I will never force the attentions of anyone on you. That is, unless you find a young man who will make you happy."

"I don't think you have to worry about me finding a young man, Jason. I'm not prepared for any relationship with a man." She glanced at the cane, which rested, at the side of her chair. Inwardly, she knew the only man she could ever love would be Russ.

* * * *

Russ left Loveland the morning after the hangings. Leaving his duties to his deputies, he promised to keep in touch with Gary and let him know as soon as he found Jesse.

Diligently, he searched hundreds of disappointing miles in every direction. Hundreds of miles of reliving the morning when the Tylers returned and tore his life to shreds.

It took almost two months for him to arrive in the small Louisiana town and stop at Madam DuPre's boarding house. He'd become discouraged, vowing if no one had seen Jesse here, he would return to Loveland, admit defeat, try to pick up what little was left of his life, and continue somehow.

"I'm looking for this girl," he told Madam DuPre, over supper. When he produced the tin plate picture he'd shown to so many others over the past several weeks, the older woman gasped.

"Are you her husband?" Her voice quivered with fear.

"Jesse has no husband," Russ replied, somewhat stunned by the words.

"Jesse?" the woman said. "Don't you mean Kate, Kate Cross?"

"Maybe that's what she called herself when you knew her, but her name is Jesse Tyler. I assume you have seen her."

"It's been over a month. I don't think I'm betraying anything by telling you."

"Betray, betray what? What did she tell you?"

"She said she was running away from her husband who beat her. All I can tell you is she left here for New Orleans. From there, who knows?"

"Was she riding a gray horse?" Russ pressed.

"She sold it, along with her rifle. She left here a very different person from when she came. When she arrived, she was a frightened, battered child. When she left, she had become an elegant lady. Only her limp and her cane distracted from her beauty. It's a shame she suffered such a tragic accident as a child."

Russ closed his eyes and imagined Jesse. An elegant lady, the woman had said. To him she had always been an elegant lady.

"Accident?" he said. "What accident are you talking about?"

"Why the riding accident when she hurt her leg, of course."

"Jesse had no accident. Have you ever heard of Caleb Tyler?" The woman's expression told him she hadn't.

Carefully, he went on to explain everything that had happened to Jesse in the past several years. When he finished, the woman wiped her tears away with a delicate lace handkerchief.

"If you are not her husband, then who are you? Are you one of them?"

Russ shook his head. "I am far from being one of them. I'm only the man who loves her. I'm the sheriff of Loveland, Missouri. As I told you earlier, my name is Russ Martin. Jesse and I were to have been married, when all this happened and she disappeared. Thank you for your help."

Russ traveled on to New Orleans, where he spoke with several people who thought they remembered Jesse. Some thought she'd taken a train East, others recalled her boarding a riverboat heading North, while still others thought she'd booked passage on a ship bound for Europe. The trail had become as cold as it could possibly get. There would never be enough time to search in every direction. Jesse had won. She'd told him she wanted to disappear and to search for her would be useless. Why hadn't he believed her?

Dejected, he returned to Loveland. It would have been easy to do as he had done after Ellie's death and pack up and leave. He could start a new life in a new town, but he knew he couldn't, wouldn't, start over. His only hope of ever seeing her again would be to stay here. If she contacted anyone, it would be Gary, and he wanted to be close enough to follow whatever lead he received.

Upon his return, he purchased Jesse's small house from the bank and moved in. He left her clothes hanging in the closet and neatly folded in the drawers, adding to them his own clothing and belongings. On the dresser, where he knew Jesse had kept his picture, he placed the photograph of her. When he did, he lovingly caressed the worn Bible she left behind.

He remembered Gary telling him how she lost her faith and her mother's Bible laying on the dresser attested to the fact. He ached, knowing how lost he'd been when he thought God no longer cared. Did Jesse feel lost? Somehow, he would have to find her and help her, as she helped him, find the road back to God.

Chapter Fifteen

May, 1892

Russ just fell asleep, or so it seemed, when he heard someone pounding on his door. He wondered what could be wrong. Quickly, he pulled on his pants and lit the lamp before answering the insistent pounding. To his surprise, Bill Carter from the telegraph office, not his deputy, stood on the porch.

"Sorry to bother you so late at night," Bill said, "but I figured you would want to see this wire right away."

Russ ripped open the envelope and read the message, almost in disbelief.

RUSS-FOUND JESSE IN VIRGINIA CITY, NEVADA-QUAID.

The words almost jumped off the paper at him.

"Thank you, Bill," he said, pumping the man's hand as he smiled broadly. "This is one wire I did want to see."

"Any reply?" Bill said, handing him a pad and pencil.

"You bet," Hastily, Russ he scribbled the reply.

QUAID-TAKING FIRST TRAIN TO VIRGINIA CITY-WILL WIRE ARRIVAL TIME-RUSS.

When Bill left, Russ found himself unable to sleep. It had been almost two years since Jesse disappeared. Every night he included her in his prayers, prayers that always ended in the same way. "Dear God, just let me find her and tell her how much I love her."

Tonight, his prayers had been answered. He couldn't believe his good fortune. Had Quaid actually found her? He wondered what he would find when he arrived in Virginia City. Did she still love him?

Once he found her, would she return with him to Loveland or would it be a futile search as she had said in her letter.

Relief encompassed his being like a warm blanket. That mingled with excitement to make sleep a stranger. Throughout the night, he wandered around the small house. When morning finally came, he made plans for the trip west.

He stopped first at his office and put things in order before going to the train station to check on train schedules. Once he did, he fingered the ticket he held in his hand. He would leave for Denver on Monday morning and, after a layover there, would arrive in Virginia City late Saturday afternoon.

After church, he sought out Gary. "I received wonderful news last evening," Russ announced. "I've found Jesse."

Gary rolled his eyes. "How many times have you said those exact same words to me over the past two years? The red haired schoolteacher in Garden City, the woman in Pecos, the nurse in New Orleans. You've followed every lead and every time you've returned empty handed and disappointed. Are you certain this time, Russ? Are you sure this isn't another wild goose chase?"

"This time the goose is real. This time I know it's Jesse."

"How can you be so positive? All those others, you were certain then, too."

"I know, but this time it's different. This time, it's as if God has told me I'll find her. You think I'm being a fool. Maybe I am, but this time the wire came from Quaid. Quaid knows Jesse."

"Quaid!" Gary exclaimed. "Isn't he in Arizona Territory or someplace like that?"

"He must have been transferred. His wire said he'd found her in Virginia City. I looked it up on the map at the train station this morning. It's out in Nevada, almost to California. My train leaves tomorrow morning. With the layover in Denver, I will be arriving Saturday afternoon."

"It's a long trip. What if she says no to you? Worse yet, what if it isn't her?"

"I've been considering those possibilities. If she says no, I can get on with my life. If it isn't her, I won't follow any more leads. I'll try to forget she ever existed."

"I wish I could go with you, but with Clara due to have the baby any day and the farm, I can't get away right now."

Russ understood and promised to keep Gary informed. He secretly wanted to travel alone, to find Jesse alone, and perhaps be disappointed alone.

Throughout the day, he thought about how things had changed and lives had gone on in the past two years. Just a year ago, Eli died suddenly. Now, the farm belonged to Clara and Gary. During that year, Gary had shown everyone what a good farmer he could be. In just over a year, he'd be a free man. Russ knew freedom would change nothing, except perhaps Gary's Saturday morning visits to his office.

Gary loved his daughter, Laura, dearly and he seemed pleased to have made the Tyler name one she could be proud of in the future. In a few more days Clara would have their second child. Russ knew Gary longed for a son.

For Gary, the past died with Caleb and Frank. Had it died for Jesse as well? Would she be able to return to Loveland with him and be happy?

He finished packing his traveling bag. As a last minute thought, he added Jesse's Bible to his clothes. If he wanted to bring her back to God, he knew she would need the security of the Bible she brought to Loveland from Clarkston.

Once on the train, his thoughts turned to Gary's concern over the false leads he'd followed. Would this be another dead end? No, Quaid wouldn't have wired if he hadn't been certain.

The closer he got to Virginia City, the more nervous he grew. He thought of the short train ride from Loveland to Clarkston when he'd first gone to bring Jesse back to him. He also thought of the letter he'd sent to the Longs just before he left for Virginia City. It sounded so optimistic, so full of hope. He'd told them he knew this time he'd found Jesse. How many other letters had he sent to them over the past two years? How many times had he written them upon his return saying the woman hadn't been Jesse? Did he have the right to continue raising their hopes, only to pull them back down?

At last, the train arrived in Virginia City. As he collected his bag, he realized how weary he'd become. He'd hardly slept. Whether it had been due to the excitement of finding Jesse, or just the movement of the train, he didn't know.

Quaid waved when he saw Russ and he returned the gesture. Quaid looked good, so smart in his uniform, with his new Lieutenant's bars on the shoulders.

"Lieutenant," Russ said, "I'm impressed, Quaid."

Quaid laughed heartily. "Battlefield promotions, but I enjoy the life. I'm glad I didn't stay on the farm."

"You'll be bucking for Captain soon," Russ teased.

"Not at this post. I'd like to stay here for a while. I like Virginia City. It's much easier duty than what I've had."

"Tell me about her, Quaid," Russ said, knowing there would be no use in making small talk. "Are you certain?"

"If this girl isn't Jesse, it's her twin sister. She's beautiful, Russ. More beautiful than I even remembered. She's an elegant lady."

Russ remembered Madam DuPre using the same words to describe the woman she'd known as Kate Cross.

Quaid remained quiet for a moment, perhaps to allow his words to have an impact on Russ. "To everyone in Virginia City, she's a mystery. I've asked a lot of questions since I saw her a week ago. I haven't received many answers, though. During the week, she deals black jack at a place called The Mother Lode, and, on Friday and Saturday nights, she sings in the restaurant. The man who runs The Mother Lode, Jason Bellinger, guards her like a hawk. They say no man but him has been to her room.

He posts around the clock bodyguards at her door. From what I've heard, they're big burly men you'd never have a chance of getting past. She calls herself Laurel Morgan and carries a silver cane. The story they tell everyone is she'd been injured in a riding accident as a child. The only time she's seen outside The Mother Lode, is on Sunday afternoons when Jason takes her out in his carriage, or they go riding. As far as anyone knows, she doesn't attend church. She does donate generously to an orphanage run by a priest for the Indian children."

Russ said nothing. Quaid's words were ones to be digested and considered before saying anything more. He'd called this woman beautiful, mysterious, well thought of, and elegant. Could she be Jesse? With Jesse's background, her Christian upbringing, could she possibly deal cards in a tavern?

"It's quite a story. Are you certain Laurel Morgan and Jesse Tyler are one in the same?"

"I've never seen another woman with hair so red or eyes so green. At first, I had doubts, but the cane, the voice, it has to be her. It can't be anyone but Jesse."

"When can I see her?" Russ said, his words hardly more than a whisper.

"She sings at seven and ten tonight. I thought maybe you would like to take dinner with me this evening at The Mother Lode."

Russ' spirits lifted. "I'd like to join you, but just how do we get to Miss Jesse?"

"I think we're going to have to do it through this Jason Bellinger."

Russ nodded and continue to listen as Quaid described the well-dressed gentleman who was the owner of the gaming club where Jesse worked.

"I reserved a room for you," Quaid finally said. "I thought you'd like to clean up a bit before we go to dinner. I'll meet you at The Mother Lode around six. Getting there an hour before her performance should give us plenty of time to have something to eat before you see her."

Chapter Sixteen

Jesse sat in front of her dressing table mirror. For two years she'd been Laurel Morgan. So much had happened in her life, she could hardly believe any of it pertained to her.

The month at Madam DuPre's followed by the trip on the riverboat had only been the beginning. Virginia City seemed like a whole other world. A world she never expected to experience.

Jason loved her. She knew he did. She also knew he'd loved her since the first moment he saw her. Otherwise he would not have taken her in the way he did. She was thankful he'd never been improper with her. When several men made advances, Jason hired bodyguards around the clock. He'd realized how terrified she became when an unknown man even approached her.

She cursed the cane she still carried. It had become a bitter reminder of the past. Because of Frank's last beating, she would probably always need it.

She pondered how different she'd become and how her life had changed. She longed for the little house at the end of Main Street. She'd been so happy there, her life so simple. She'd run the shop, been respected, loved Russ, and found comfort in the worn Bible. Would she ever find comfort in those words again? Would she ever be able to love Russ or anyone else? The answers to both questions eluded her. God, like Russ, would never be able to forgive her. It seemed best for Jesse to remain dead and for Laurel to continue her sheltered life.

As she looked at her freshly scrubbed face in the mirror, she longed to see Laurel Morgan. Instead, Jesse Tyler stared at her, accusingly.

"Can't you go away?" she said to the reflection. "Can't you go

116

quietly away like Kate Cross? Can't you disappear and be no more?"

The face mocked her. In her heart, she heard a voice. "I can't go away from you, for I am you, and you are me. You've hurt so many people you have to make it up to them."

She understood the reason behind the voice. She knew she had to return to Loveland and Clarkston, but her fear of returning kept her in Virginia City. No matter what Gary promised or what Russ said, she had to pay for her crime. Would anyone have compassion for a woman who tried to kill her own father?

For no reason, she began to cry. Tears spilled from her eyes at such a pace, she found once she started she couldn't stop. Silent sobs shook her body until she heard a knock at the door.

Wiping her eyes, she finally managed to speak. "Who is it?"

"It's Jason, Laurel."

"Just a moment," she replied, pulling on her dressing gown. She didn't bother to get up to answer the door. She knew it wasn't necessary. Jason posed no threat to her. He always entered her room after knocking, so she wouldn't have to get up from her chair.

"What's wrong, Laurel?" He placed his hands on her shoulders to massage the tension from her neck. "You've been crying."

She pointed to the mirror. "She's what's wrong. I'm what's wrong."

"Is Jesse haunting you?"

Her eyes went wide as they met his in the mirror. "You know?"

"Yes."

"How long have you known?" Her words were those of disbelief.

"I've always know. Good grief, Laurel, I would have had to be blind and deaf not to have known who you were. Even in New Orleans the papers were full of Caleb Tyler and his beautiful red headed daughter with green eyes. They made quite a thing about how she shot him and then disappeared without a trace. The instant I saw you, I knew."

Memories flooded her mind as tears washed her face. "You never let on or told anyone about Laurel Morgan's past. Why? You must have known people were looking for me."

"Everyone has a past, my dear. If you wanted your past buried, I didn't have the right to dig it up."

"Everyone, Jason? Even you?"

"Even me."

"Tell me about it." She longed to know someone other than herself had something to hide."

"Someday, Laurel. Someday, when I can come to grips with it, myself. I'm not ready to face it, even after twenty years. I'm afraid you are ready to face Jesse, though. When you do, I will certainly lose you."

"Lose me? What do you mean? Where would I go? What would I do?"

"Perhaps you'd go home, back to your brother and the man in your picture."

"What do you know about him? I've never mentioned him to anyone."

"I knew he wasn't your brother as you told me. I also knew he'd been special to you. If not, you would have put the picture away long ago."

"Why did you help me, Jason? Why have you protected me, knowing who I am?"

Jason put his hand to her cheek. "You were so frightened, so vulnerable. I couldn't let you end up with the wrong people, living out your life in someone's upstairs bedroom. You were special, so I created you to be special. The silver cane, the bodyguards, the clothes, everything has been my creation. You are my creation. To say otherwise would be a lie. You've earned me more money than anyone else who has ever sung here. I'm selfish enough to protect you and hope you won't ever leave me."

She wiped her eyes again. "What if someday Laurel Morgan wants to be Jesse Tyler again?"

"Then I ask she not forget me, and she keeps in touch. Do you want to be Jesse Tyler again?"

"I gave up so much to be Laurel Morgan and yet I'm afraid to be Jesse Tyler. As Jesse, I'd fallen in love with a wonderful man. I see now he deserves better than Caleb Tyler's daughter."

"The man on your dresser."

"Yes. His name is Russ Martin, and I loved him."

"Do you still love him?"

"I think I'll always love him, but it's an impossible dream. Russ is the sheriff of Loveland, and Loveland is where I shot Pa. I'm certain he doesn't love me anymore, certain he only wants to arrest me."

Jason shook his head. "What if I could find him? Would it make you happy again? I hate to see you cry. You know I'd move heaven and earth for you. Just say the word and I'll send him a wire. I'll ask him to come here."

"Thank you, Jason. It's a beautiful thought, and I love you for it, but I'm afraid he wouldn't come. All I ever wanted was to be loved. I've hurt everyone I love. Don't let me hurt you as well. Help me forget Jesse Tyler ever existed."

"Help you? How?"

"Don't stop loving me."

"Am I so obvious?"

Jesse managed to smile through her tears. "Yes, but I don't mind. If you didn't love me, you wouldn't protect me and there would be no guards at my door. If you didn't love me the way you do, I'd no longer be..." She paused for a moment. Good girls didn't profess their virginity, even to someone they cared deeply for. "Oh, it doesn't matter. I think you see me as your little girl."

Jason smiled. "Then you're not leaving?"

"Not right away. Help me make the right decision."

"I'm afraid if I help you, the decision will be not to ever leave Virginia City. If I had my way, Laurel Morgan would always continue to shine brighter than all the stars in the heavens."

Jason bent to kiss her neck before leaving to begin the evening with greeting his dinner guests.

Jesse watched him leave and wondered if his love for her could be called the love of a father for a daughter, or if it were more. She trusted him, but she could never love him as she did Russ. If she decided to remain Laurel Morgan, she'd be forced to decide what to do about Jason. The only logical thing for her to do would be to marry him, and yet, she didn't love him the way a wife should love her husband.

"Whatever are you going to do, Laurel?" she said the mirror. "If you stay here and marry Jason, you'll be denying every feeling Jesse ever had for Russ. If you go back to Loveland, you face losing your precious freedom. If that were the case, you would be hurting the one person who has befriended you, loved you, and created you. I wish it were an easier decision, but it isn't. Maybe someday you'll find the answer, the solution to everything without hurting anyone."

Maybe the solution is in the past. What gave you the most comfort when you were growing up, when you were riding with Caleb, when you were trying to decide how to answer Russ when he asked you to marry him?

Jesse shook her head in an attempt to make the voice go away. She knew the answer. The answer was God, but He had ceased to exist for her. There would be no forgiveness, no welcoming for Jesse Tyler. She'd ridden with and shot Caleb. Now she sang in a place where gambling and liquor went hand in hand.

"No," she said aloud. "I can't find comfort in God, because I'm not good enough to ask for His forgiveness. I'll never be able to be Jesse Tyler again. She must die, just as Kate Cross died. Only Laurel Morgan exists. She will have to be enough for me."

Chapter Seventeen

Russ accompanied Quaid to The Mother Lode. When they entered, he saw an older man greeting the guests.

"I enjoyed last Saturday evening's performance very much," Quaid said, shaking Jason Bellinger's hand. "Since my friend happened to be in Virginia City on business, I knew he would enjoy it as well."

"Welcome to The Mother Lode, Mr...." Jason extended his hand.

"Martin, Russell Martin," Russ replied. As he shook hands with the man, he fought the urge to demand to be taken to Jesse's room. "Quaid tells me I'm in for a special treat this evening. He's certain I'll enjoy not only the food, but the entertainment as well."

"Well I do hope we can live up to the stories the young Lieutenant has been telling you. Perhaps after the show, we can interest you in some of our games of chance. Are you a gambling man?"

"You might say so," Russ replied, smiling broadly. He was gambling on finding Jesse and winning her back.

The smile on Jason's face confused Russ. He wondered if Jason were smiling because he thought Russ would gamble away all of his money, or because Russ threatened him. Russ dismissed the latter. Jason Bellinger could, in no way, know what kind of a threat Russ posed.

"What do you suggest tonight, Mr. Bellinger?" Quaid said.

"The trout. It was caught fresh this morning," Jason replied, playing the perfect host. "I'd usually recommend the steak, but tonight the trout is excellent."

Once they were escorted to a table, Quaid ordered a bottle of wine. Russ wasn't surprised. Even though his drinking had dwindled to almost nothing before he left Loveland, Russ knew how hard old habits were to break. The selection of wine surprised him. He could only hope Quaid did his drinking in more moderation than he had four years earlier.

Russ knew Quaid recognized the look of apprehension on his face, when he said, "I indulge in wine on special occasions. I've grown up a lot, Russ. Whiskey isn't as important to me as it used to be."

Russ breathed a sigh of relief. "I'm glad to hear it. Whiskey can wreck your life. If you recall, it almost got your whole family killed when Jesse stayed with you. You can be thankful Gary overheard you in the tavern and not Frank or Caleb."

"Don't think for a minute, the thought doesn't cross my mind at least once a week. What were they like? I've often wondered."

"They were exactly as Gary and Jesse described them at Gary's trial. Cold, ruthless, unable to believe what they'd done with their lives was wrong. Seeing them hang brought relief for me, but it took its toll on Gary. Of course, before they even came to trial, Jesse left town. She couldn't face them, couldn't stay knowing what they were and what they'd done. They injured her so badly, I don't know how she found the strength to ride all the way to Louisiana. Did you say she still uses a cane?"

"Yes. Her limp is very pronounced, but she's still beautiful. More beautiful, I think, than four years ago."

They talked on for several more minutes. Each word made Russ wonder if he'd done the right thing in coming to Virginia City. Jesse ran away from him once and had considered it one other time. Would she even want to see him now?

When the trout was served, both Russ and Quaid had to admit it was as excellent as Jason promised. They'd just finished eating when Jason took the stage.

"Ladies and gentlemen, for your entertainment, The Mother Lode proudly presents, Miss Laurel Morgan."

Russ gasped at the sight of Laurel on the stage. Quaid was right, she was Jesse. There could be absolutely no doubt about it. She wore a green dress overlaid with a sheer silvery netting, showing just a hint of cleavage and satiny white shoulders. Around her neck, she wore a silver necklace with a single emerald, and matching earrings graced her delicate lobes.

His heart pounded as he listened to her sing. Closing his eyes, he could see her standing in front of the small church in Clarkston, her hair loose, her face freshly scrubbed, singing to the congregation on Easter Sunday morning, three years earlier. He sat close enough to reach her in a matter of a few steps and yet he was rooted to the spot, unable to move. Only the explosion of applause woke him to the fact Jesse had been escorted from the stage.

"Well," Quaid said, "what do you think? Was I wrong to send you the wire?"

"It's Jesse. You weren't wrong, but I'm not certain I had the right to come. Did you see her, the gown, and the jewels? How can I compete with those? How can I ask her to give all of this up? I can't offer her such things in Loveland. She'd be a fool to leave all of this behind for me."

Quaid's expression said he couldn't believe Russ' words. "Are you telling me you came all this way, and you don't intend to see her?"

Before Russ could answer, Jason stood at their table. "Well, Mr. Martin, is she the woman you came to find?"

"What do you mean?" Russ said, wondering how this stranger could possibly know why he'd come to Virginia City.

"I know you came here to find Jesse Tyler. Did you find her?"

"I'm not sure. How did you know I came here to find Jesse?"

"You, like Laurel, underestimate me. If I hadn't recognized your name, I would have known you from the picture on her dresser. Do you want to meet her?"

"I think I do. I've made a long trip from Loveland for that reason. I'd be a fool to turn tail now."

"Then come with me, gentlemen." Jason led the way to the winding staircase, which would take them to the upper floor.

* * * *

Jesse looked into the dressing table mirror and to her relief, Laurel Morgan stared back at her. Tonight's performance had been perfection. The cheers and the applause rang in her ears. Her earlier tears were gone, replaced by the sparkle of excitement.

Had she finally laid Jesse to rest? Her gaze fell on Russ' picture. No,

Jesse will never be at rest. Perhaps the time has come for Laurel, like Kate, to be put behind her.

Just the thought of giving up everything she'd worked so hard to achieve in Virginia City, distressed her. If she was no longer Laurel Morgan, who would she become?

She contemplated writing to Russ, but what would she say? She couldn't tell him where she lived, and yet, she couldn't tell him why she left either. Knowing Jason was aware of her identity, she knew it would only be a matter of time before Russ found her. Without any other option, she reached for a pencil and paper.

Dear Russ,
    I love you, but I've hurt you so badly. I've gone against
your wishes. I know you could never love me, knowing what
I've become.

She crumpled the paper. She couldn't say those things. It hurt too much even to think them and writing them hurt even more. She was content to be Laurel for as long as Jason wanted. Let Russ, Gary, and everyone else believe she was dead. It was for the best.

* * * *

Russ and Quaid followed Jason up the stairs and watched as he dismissed the man who stood outside Jesse's door. "I want to see Miss Laurel alone. I've brought her some visitors."

The man assessed Russ and Quaid, his eyes showing doubt at Jason's decision to let them into Miss Laurel's room. "Are you sure, Mr. Bellinger?"

"Yes, Jake, I'm sure. Nothing will happen to her."

Russ watched the man go down the stairs, glancing over his shoulder to see if Jason had been forced to take these strangers into Miss Laurel's room

Why did Jesse need a guard at her door? Did Jason think she was in danger, or did he think she'd run away from Virginia City as she did from Loveland?

"Why the bodyguard?" Russ finally said, unable to resist voicing the question that stood foremost in his mind

"Laurel is a frightened child," Jason replied.

"She didn't look frightened to me," Russ said, flatly.

"On stage, she's very sure of herself. She's in control. When she's alone, things are different. No man touches her. I see to that."

"Except you?" Russ said, knowing the question to be improper.

"Not even me. It became an important part of our agreement when we first met. Her beauty, elegance, and talent, in exchange for my protection. I don't plan to deceive you, Mr. Martin, I love Laurel because I created her. I would do anything in my power to make her happy."

Russ wanted to believe Jason, wanted to think of Jesse as unblemished as she'd been when she left Loveland, but he couldn't. Too much had happened to leave her unscathed.

Jason knocked at Jesse's door, and Russ held his breath, anxious to hear her voice.

"Jason, come in, please come in," she called. She sounded more like an excited child than the elegant lady he'd seen only moments ago on stage.

Russ wished she would move into his line of vision. The sound of her voice only teased him. He wanted to hold her and tell her how much he loved her. If Jason hadn't motioned for him to wait with Quaid, he would have followed him into the room.

Through the partially open door, Russ watched as Jesse stood beside her dressing table to hug Jason, then kiss him lightly on the cheek. For the first time, he experienced pains of jealousy. He wanted to be the one Jesse clung to for reassurance, the one she kissed.

"Oh, Jason," she said, her voice becoming soft and melodious. "Wasn't it wonderful? Did you hear the applause?"

"Yes, Laurel, they loved you. They always love you."

"It has to be considered one of the best performances I've ever given," she continued.

"Maybe I have the reason it seemed so special with me. I've brought you a visitor, someone very special."

Jesse laughed, a light laugh, hardly more than a giggle, more like one of disbelief. "Be serious, Jason, you never bring me visitors."

"This person has come a long way, Laurel, a very long way to find

Jesse."

Russ watched as the color drained from her face and her eyes became those of a frightened child. "Oh, Jason, no. Who could have found me? Is it Russ? Oh no, it can't be Russ!" Her voice, like her eyes changed from excitement to despair.

Hearing the words, Russ' head began to spin. He knew his heart would break if he stayed here any longer listening to the terror in her voice. As though the past four years hadn't happened. He could hear the same fear he'd heard in the bedroom of the McPhearson home. The same fear he'd heard at Gary's trial. The same fear he'd heard when he begged to see her just before she left Loveland.

"You stay, Quaid. You explain it to her. I can't," he said, turning toward the staircase.

Quaid caught Russ' arm. "Wait."

"For what? To have her tell me to my face she doesn't want to see me? I don't think so." He pulled away and hurried down the stairs.

* * * *

"You're going to see him, Laurel," Jason said, his voice firm.

"Please, Jason, don't make me do this," she protested, her heart pounding wildly in her chest. "I can't see him. I can't stand to—"

"What are you afraid of?" Jason said interrupting her. The tone of his voice had raised noticeably.

"Even if I could explain it, you'd never understand."

"Maybe I would."

Jesse turned to see Quaid enter the room. Just seeing this ghost from her past frightened her.

"What kind of game are you playing? Mr. Bellinger says you keep Russ' picture on your dresser. Now when he's right outside your door, you don't want to see him."

"Quaid?" she said, still having problems believing he actually stood in front of her.

"How do you think he found you? I saw you last Saturday evening. I sent him a wire. He's been looking for you for months."

"Looking for me to arrest me," Jesse said, flatly.

Quaid put his hands on her shoulders. "Is that what you think? Is that why you won't see him? He's been searching for you for the past two years. He's followed every lead. He wants to take you back home, where you belong. He loves you, Jesse."

"Where did he go?"

Quaid shook his head. "I don't know. He's hurt, terribly hurt."

She grabbed her cane and pushed past him. I have to find him."

Chapter Eighteen

Russ hurried down the stairs, past the man he'd seen outside Jesse's room, and out the front door. Just down the street stood a tavern, a real tavern, not some fancy pants gaming club.

Inside The Gilded Lily, he knew there would be girls who'd welcome him rather than fear him. The girls could wait. Right now he needed a drink. There would be time to enjoy the companionship of a lady later in the evening.

Two years, two years he'd longed for Jesse, and the minute she heard his name all the old fears returned. She wanted nothing to do with him. His coming here had been wrong.

Once inside the brightly lit tavern, he pulled a twenty-dollar gold piece from his pocket and laid it on the bar. "I want a bottle and a glass. I want it to be the best and when that is gone I want another, and another after that until the money is gone."

"Yes, sir," the bartender replied, handing him a bottle and a shot glass.

Before he even left the bar, a pretty young girl came over and put her arm around his neck. "You wouldn't mind sharing, would you?" Her voice dripping with insincere sweetness.

"Why not? Bartender, give me another glass," Russ replied, putting his arm around the girl's waist and nuzzling her sweet smelling neck.

A voice in his head told him his actions were wrong. It continued to say they went against everything he held dear, his love for Jesse as well as his faith. Hurt and angry, he refused to listen. He'd come to believe in the God Jesse believed in. He'd returned to the faith he'd enjoyed as a child as well as when he and Ellie had been so happy, but what had it gotten him. The one person in his life who mattered had openly said she didn't want to see him. How could God be so cruel?

It had been years since he'd wanted a drink, years since he thought whiskey could make things appear clearer. Now he wondered why he hadn't taken to the bottle earlier. He had cause, everyone knew he had cause. Everyone except God. Had his faith kept him away from the pleasures of the flesh for these past two years?

Rather than continue to dwell on it, he turned his attentions to the young girl. Once they sat at one of the tables, he poured a drink for himself as well as one for her. With all his heart, he hoped she'd drive Jesse from his mind. Roughly he kissed her, but he could muster no feelings other than repulsion. She wasn't Jesse. She could never be Jesse. He'd kissed a stranger, someone who kissed several different men a night, someone who tried to drive the hurts away, but never really succeeded.

"What brings you to Virginia City, honey?" she asked, her finger tracing around his ear.

Her actions took him a bit by surprise, even though he knew she made her living entertaining men. He realized he didn't like her, didn't want her to touch him in such a way.

"A funeral," he said, gently placing her hand on the table.

"I'm real sorry, honey," she whispered, her lips brushing against his cheek.

He pushed her away in disgust. "You want to drink, then drink. I don't want to talk anymore."

* * * *

Jesse's mind whirled as she hurried as fast as she could down the hall and made her way clumsily down the stairs. Jake met her at the first landing.

"Miss Laurel, what's wrong? You're cryin'."

"Yes, Jake, I'm crying."

"Then let me help you."

"Please Jake, please don't. I'll be all right. I need to be alone for a while is all."

"Mr. Jason won't be real happy about you bein' alone."

"Mr. Jason isn't happy about a lot of things lately. I'll be fine. You won't lose your job."

Several guests tried to speak to her as she hurried through the dining room, but she ignored them. She couldn't be polite. She had to find Russ. She had to explain, to tell him she still loved him.

Dave Bellows stood at his customary place at the door and opened it for her as she approached. "Miss Laurel, it's a pleasure to see you. Why isn't Jake with you?"

"Can't anyone understand? I want to be alone for a few minutes. Is it such a crime?"

"Of course not," Dave replied, concern in his voice.

"Good. A man just left here alone. He came in with a young Lieutenant earlier. Did you see him?"

"Yes, Miss Laurel. He went to The Gilded Lily."

"Thank you, Dave." She turned to enter the darkness of the evening and cross the street to the tavern."

"Miss Laurel," Dave said, causing her to stop. "You can't—"

"Yes, Dave, I can. I can handle myself better than any of you ever thought I could."

"You shouldn't go to a place like The Gilded Lily alone. Let me get Mr. Bellinger or Jake to go with you."

"I'm sick to death of Mr. Bellinger. He knows what I'm doing. He's responsible for it."

"But you can't go there," Dave again protested.

Jesse didn't turn back at his words. Whatever anyone said, at this point had lost its meaning. Russ became the only thing she cared about. She needed to see him to try to make amends for the past. To her surprise, the hot tears, which cascaded down her cheeks, stood in direct contrast to the chill of the evening. The sudden cold caused her to shake, and she wished she'd taken a shawl.

The last few days had been difficult. She realized it now. Perhaps she'd been preparing herself for this confrontation without even knowing it. She'd had very little sleep although she hadn't told Jason. She knew he would scold her and insist she see the doctor.

Tonight's performance had been exhilarating, but the realization Russ had been there drained her. She experienced an overwhelming sense of exhaustion and the familiar dizziness that accompanied it. It had all been Frank's fault. The last beating when she hit her head had taken her strength. Since then the dizziness came often although she told no one about it.

A few doors down the street, she saw the lights and heard the noisy din coming from The Gilded Lily. Everyone had been right, it was no place for a woman alone, especially not for Laurel Morgan. It appeared to be a wild and rowdy place, but if Russ had gone to The Gilded Lily, so would she. She loved him too much not to see him. She wanted to believe Quaid, to believe Russ came because he loved her. If he arrested her, so be it. She no longer cared. A prison with bars would be acceptable after the prison she'd kept Jesse in for so very long. Laurel Morgan's life resembled a fairy tale, Jesse Tyler's life a nightmare. She had to atone for her sins.

Dear God, just let him be there. She stopped her prayer short. It was the first time she'd prayed in two years. Looking heavenward, the stars seemed to shine a little brighter. The load of Jesse's guilt lifted slightly from her shoulders.

"I should have given it to You long ago," she said aloud. "No matter what, You'll see me through this ordeal."

Taking a deep breath, she stepped through the swinging doors, into the smoky room. This rowdy tavern was no place for Laurel Morgan, but Jesse Tyler stood there defiantly.

The man playing the piano saw her and stopped playing abruptly. Conversations ceased, and the man behind the bar recognized and acknowledged her.

"Why, Miss Laurel, can I get you a table?"

"No thank you," she replied, in her sweetest Laurel Morgan voice, bestowing on him one of her famous Laurel Morgan smiles. It was a smile, she knew, most men would die for. "I'm looking for someone. I was told he came in here."

Russ sat about three tables from her, a pretty girl beside him. "Well, well, well," he said, as he stood and started toward her. "If it isn't Jesse Tyler. Or is it Kate Cross? Or perhaps it's Laurel Morgan?"

Tears stung Jesse's eyes, and she began to shake uncontrollably. The harshness of Russ' voice and the coldness of his eyes hurt her deeply.

131

"Laurel Morgan would not be here without a chaperone and Kate Cross is dead."

To her surprise, Russ began to applaud her. "So are you Jesse Tyler, or is there someone else I don't know about?"

Jesse's eyes darted from Russ' face, the face she'd loved so deeply for the past three years, to the half-empty bottle on the table. Russ was drunk. Drunk like she'd seen Caleb and Frank so many times. Inside she shivered, fearing the unknown. Had she been responsible for this? She knew Russ didn't drink.

"I'm Jesse, Russ, no one else, not tonight. I've come here to find you, to tell you.—"

Russ cut her short. "I'm sorry, Jesse, those are my words, the things I came here to say to you." As he spoke, he moved to her side.

He stood so close to her she could smell the whiskey mingled with the scent of the after-shave she remembered he always used. Without warning, he grabbed her arm and held it in a vice like grip. Looking into his eyes, she could see Frank.

"You're hurting me," she whispered.

"Is that supposed to make me feel bad?" he said. His voice no longer belonged to the man she loved. It had become a mixture of Frank's voice and the slurred ramblings of a drunk.

"No," she said, hardly loud enough for him to hear. Her eyes pleaded with him to stop.

She only wanted to find Russ, Russ as she remembered him, not Russ like this. He was accusing her. He didn't come here to profess his love. He came to arrest her, to make her atone for the sin she committed in Loveland. Why did Quaid ever get stationed in Virginia City? Why couldn't the past remain dead? Why couldn't she go on being Laurel Morgan and forget Jesse Tyler ever existed?

"We're going to go someplace to talk, Jesse, just you and me." Russ's voice broke into her thoughts.

As he turned, pushing her toward the door, she caught the glimpse of metal as the bartender pulled a shotgun from behind the bar.

"I wouldn't try it, Mister, not with Miss Laurel."

"Can't you see, there is no Laurel Morgan," Russ shouted. "There's only Jesse Tyler. Maybe you don't know about her, but I do."

"Russ, please," she pleaded, as his grip became tighter. She turned to the bartender. "It's all right."

"No, it ain't, Miss Laurel. I'm sendin' a man over to The Mother Lode to fetch someone to take you home."

Russ stared into her eyes. "Is The Mother Lode home now, Jesse? Do you call a tavern home, when you could have had so much more?"

Before she could answer, Jake appeared. Catching Russ off guard, Jake knocked him to the floor with one blow.

Jesse sobbed hysterically, as she sank to her knees at Russ' side. "What have you done, Jake?" she said, recoiling as he touched her, crying as he helped her to her feet before collapsing, exhausted, into his strong arms.

* * * *

Russ could feel someone slapping his face and hear Quaid calling his name.

"What hit me?" he mumbled, rubbing his bloodied cheek. "A Missouri Mule? It sure felt like one."

He saw Quaid wrinkle his nose at the smell of whiskey on his breath. "Now it's my turn, Russ. Don't you know whiskey can ruin your life? What happened?"

"I got upset. I don't know why I thought getting drunk would make everything clearer, but I did. It had to have been the whiskey talking. I grabbed Jesse's arm and told her we had to go somewhere to talk, alone. I'd planned to take her to my room at the hotel and make her tell me the truth about why she left Loveland. The next thing I knew, the bartender pulled a gun on me, and that big ox came through the door. When I came to, you were slapping me silly." Russ switched his gaze from Quaid and searched the room.

"If you're looking for Laurel," Jason said, moving into Russ' line of vision, "I had Jake take her back to The Mother Lode. She collapsed, and I wanted her to be checked by a doctor."

Russ shook his head to clear his mind, as Quaid helped him to his feet. "I have a knack for making things worse, don't I?" The fact he had trouble regaining his balance forced him to lean heavily against Quaid for support.

Jason looked relieved to see a large black man appear at the door.

"We have another casualty, Sam. Take him over to The Mother Lode and put him in the room next to Miss Laurel."

The black man took Russ' arm. "Just take me back to my hotel," Russ protested, trying to pull away from the black man's grip.

"Mr. Jason said you're to go back to The Mother Lode," Sam said, his voice softer, more gentle than anyone would have expected. "You need someone to take care of your face. Jake said he hurt you bad. He's not very smart, and he certainly doesn't know his own strength."

"There's no use in arguing with the man, Russ," Quaid said. "I'll pick up your things at the hotel, settle up your bill, and meet you at The Mother Lode. I agree with Jason and Sam, you need to have a doctor look at your face."

Chapter Nineteen

Jesse lay on the bed. The green and silver dress looked less elegant than it had earlier. As her eyes fluttered open, she saw Sally, her maid, with a worried expression on her face.

"You had me worried half to death, child," Sally proclaimed.

"Sally? Where's Russ?"

"Who?"

"Russ. Jason told me he came here. I have to see him. I just have to see him," she pleaded, tears running down her cheeks.

"I don't know who you're talkin' about, child. You're not gonna see no one until the doctor gets here."

"You don't understand, Sally. Russ is here. The man in my picture has come to find me. I have to see him. I said some terrible things. I have to tell him..." she stopped short. What did she have to tell him? Could she ever convince him she loved him? Could she ever make up for what she did in Loveland, of for what she said only a few minutes ago?

The woman patted her hand. "You have to get some rest, child. When I know you're gonna to be all right, we'll talk to Mr. Jason about it."

Jesse knew better than to argue with Sally. They had been friends ever since Jason insisted Sally become Jesse's maid. In reality, the woman was more of a mother hen than a hired servant.

Dr. Carrier arrived, and took Jesse's wrist in his hand. "Well, Miss Morgan, I never thought you would become my patient. I'm honored. Why don't you tell me what happened tonight?"

"Happened?" Jesse said, horrified and confused.

"At The Gilded Lily," Dr. Carrier prompted.

"That can't be," she gasped, her heart pounding wildly with terror. "I've never been within a hundred feet of The Gilded Lily in my life." Jesse began to shake, unable to control either the tremors wracking her body or the tears that rolled down her cheeks.

"Calm down, Miss Morgan. Everything is all right. Just tell me what you do remember of your activities tonight."

Jesse thought for a moment, then began, slowly. "Jason told me Russ had arrived. Quaid told me Russ loved me. I panicked and went to find him. I went downstairs. I remember the stars and the cold. I remember praying God would let me find Russ, and..." her voice trailed off as a curtain pulled across her memory.

"Do you remember anything else?"

Jesse shook her head.

"Do you remember how you were feeling?"

She closed her eyes. "Tired, very tired. I get dizzy when I get tired."

"Why haven't you ever come to my office and told me about the dizziness?"

"I know what it's from and how to avoid it," Jesse replied.

"Would you like to tell me about it?"

Jesse ran her tongue over her lips as she weighed her answer. "Before I became Laurel Morgan, my live was very different. I suffered several severe beatings at the hands of my older brother and my father. My brother gave me one last beating, a farewell gift you might say. I became extremely confused and, although the doctor took care of me after it happened, I chose to disappear without allowing him to see me again."

"What about your vision, your speech, have they ever bothered you?" Dr. Carrier pressed.

"When I'm not tired, they're fine. When I'm tired, my speech slurs and my vision becomes blurry, like it is now." Jesse saw the concern in the doctor's eyes. "I'll save you your next question. It doesn't happen often. Jason doesn't allow me to become overly tired. He does this because he thinks it's best for me. He has no idea of what happens when I don't get enough rest. I've never told him. It would only worry him, unnecessarily. Am I terribly ill? Will I die?"

"Perhaps I should tell you not to get tired, but it seems you've been doing the things I would suggest ever since you arrived in Virginia City two years ago. For now, you're not going to die, but you are going to rest. I want to do some further checking on your condition. To do that, you must tell me more about it."

Jesse stared into Dr. Carrier's eyes and tried to smile weakly. "Maybe if I face up to my past, it would help. Laurel Morgan has an ugly past life to face. Until tonight, I thought if I kept it all buried, it would go away and never haunt me."

"Do you want to tell me about it?"

"No. Jason knows all about Laurel Morgan's past. He can tell you about her."

"You talk as though Laurel Morgan doesn't exist."

"She doesn't. Until two years ago there was no Laurel Morgan. She's only Jesse Tyler using a different name in a different city, the way she has before." She lay back against the pillow, giving into the exhaustion, which plagued her and the tears, which wouldn't stop.

"I want you to rest. I'm going to give you something for sleep. I plan to sit right here until you drink it. I can tell by the look in your eyes, you don't take orders well."

"Can I please see Russ first?"

"There will be plenty of time to see whomever you want, once you rest. I'm certain Jason will cater to your every need."

Without further conversation, he helped her drink the medication. As she fell asleep, she was aware of him sitting next to the bed, holding her hand.

* * * *

Russ lay on the bed. His head ached from the whiskey, his face ached from the blow he'd received from Jake.

"Go ahead and say it," he finally said.

"Say what?" Quaid replied.

"I made a fool out of myself tonight. What more is there to say?"

"I don't know. Maybe you could say you let your emotions take over your mind. Whatever possessed you to go to The Gilded Lily in the first place? I never knew you to be a drinking man, especially after Ma said you joined the church and all."

Russ hung his head. His actions tonight embarrassed him. Jesse led him back to the Lord. She'd been patient when his journey took longer than either of them ever thought it would. Now when Jesse needed him the most to help her rediscover her faith, he'd let her down. He tried to forget everything that mattered to him by losing himself inside a bottle.

"I can't give you an answer, Quaid. I don't know why I thought I could make everything go away by drowning myself in whiskey."

After a light rap on the door, Dr. Carrier entered the room. As he did, Russ could see a look of relief cross Quaid's face.

"Now that I know there's a doctor here, I'd best be going," Quaid said, shaking Russ' hand. "I need to get back to the fort."

"Thanks for everything, Quaid. I hope I'll see you again before I leave."

"Before you take Jesse back to Loveland," Quaid corrected him.

"Before I leave," Russ replied, flatly.

Chapter Twenty

Jesse woke, wishing Russ would be sitting next to her bed when she opened her eyes. She knew it was foolish to contemplate such a thing. She had no memory of last evening's events. Had Russ come to Virginia City to profess his love, to arrest her, to get revenge, or had she dreamed the entire thing?

The cutting words she remembered speaking echoed in her mind and she knew it had been no dream. A nightmare no doubt, but no dream.

She could hear her own voice saying, "No, not Russ!" She hadn't meant the words the way they came out. They'd sounded terrible. She'd sounded terrible. Could she be such a horrid person? She hoped not and yet she didn't know. She no longer knew herself. Was she Jesse, defiant, hurt Jesse; or Kate, uncertain, wounded Kate; or had she indeed become Laurel, elegant, frightened Laurel?

One memory remained, the memory of praying, really praying. The words had sounded so alien when she first spoke them, but even now, she had begun to feel a new sense of peace. Could she let God back into her life? Would He ever be able to forgive her?

She knew someone sat next to her bed. She could hear breathing and smelled Jason's cologne. Opening her eyes, she saw Jason break into a smile.

"Good morning, Sleeping Beauty," he greeted her, taking her hand in his.

"Good morning," she replied. "Have you been here all night?"

"Most of it. You gave us all quite a scare last evening, Laurel."

"I don't know if you should call me Laurel. I don't know who or what I am. I don't even know what I should say to you."

"Then say nothing. You're going to be fine. I've been wrong to let you believe I never knew who you were. Perhaps if I'd confronted you with Jesse immediately, none of this would have happened. I blame myself as much as anyone."

"I wish you wouldn't do that. None of this has been your fault. It all happened long before you ever met me. What about Russ? Is he here, or did I only imagine it?"

"He's here, and you'll see him, when the time is right."

"Because you'll make him see me, or because he wants to see me?" She spoke, knowing it would hurt Jason, but with the realization, she needed to say it and needed to know the answer.

"He's in the next room," Jason said, his voice sounding sadder than she'd ever heard it before.

"Because he wants to be here or because you're catering to my needs as you always do?"

She watched as Jason cringed at her words. "He's here because a lot went on last night at The Gilded Lily."

"I don't remember any of it. Maybe it's best I don't."

"Let me finish. Russ decided he'd take you to his hotel room to talk. The bartender thought he wanted to kidnap you."

"KIDNAP ME?" Jesse echoed his words, her eyes widening with shock.

"Look at the bruise on your arm. Russ had been drinking, and he grabbed you."

Jesse looked at her upper arm in disbelief and rubbed the bruise that had formed there. "It looks like the bruises Frank used to give me."

"He's hurt," Jason continued. "Hurt and angry, but you'll see it for yourself. The bartender pulled a gun and, before anything further happened, Jake came in. He thought you were being hurt. When I got there he'd knocked Russ unconscious."

"Jake hit him?" she interrupted.

"Jake loves you, too. He doesn't know his own strength, though. Russ' cheek had been split open. I had him brought back here where we could keep an eye on him."

"Is he all right?"

"He's suffering from a bad case of wounded pride. I would imagine

140

his face will be sore for a while, but he'll be all right."

"And Jake?"

"He feels badly, especially when he realized just who Russ Martin is and what he means to you."

"I have to talk to him. He only did his job."

"I know you will, but not just yet." Jason sat silently for a moment. "What about you, Laurel?"

"I don't know. My first thought when I woke up had been to run away, change my name, and disappear. I can't keep on running, Jason. It makes no sense."

Jason smiled. "Thank goodness for small favors. I couldn't stand not knowing where you were. Are you going back to Loveland with Russ?"

"He hasn't asked me. If he does, I don't know if I can face going back there."

"Don't you still have a brother living in Loveland?"

"Yes, but Caleb and Frank are there as well."

"They're dead, Laurel."

"Are they? Not to me. I see them whenever I close my eyes. How could I ever stay in the house where I last saw them, where I shot Caleb? I love it here in Virginia City, although I don't know if I can ever be Laurel Morgan again, if I can continue singing. I do know Jesse Tyler can never go back to Loveland for anything but a visit."

"What about Russ?"

"I don't know. I'm so scared about him. What if I lose him?"

"Whatever happens will be for the best, I promise you," Jason said, reassuringly.

"What if he doesn't want to see me? Can you still say it will be for the best?"

Jason laughed out loud at the irony of her statement. "The man has come a thousand miles to see you. That's the one thing about Jesse Tyler I don't like."

"What do you mean?"

"She doesn't think very highly of herself."

"She's never had a reason to," Jesse snapped.

"Laurel thinks very highly of herself," Jason pressed.

"Laurel is very shallow. She thinks only of herself.

"I wouldn't say that, but I won't argue with you. Why don't we put the two of them together? Laurel would have never set foot inside The Gilded Lily last night, and yet Jesse went storming in after the man she loves."

"I wish I could remember it. I do remember I love him, but I didn't think—"

"I've always known you love him. I've kept hoping you would put his picture away and love me in the same way. Somehow I knew it would never happen."

A knock at the door interrupted him. "That must be Sally with your breakfast. After you've eaten, she'll help you with your bath. When you're ready, I'll send Russ up to see you."

* * * *

Russ woke slowly, not knowing what hurt the most, his face where the stitches held his cheek together or his head from last night's whiskey. It had been ten years since he'd sat at a table and deliberately tried to get drunk. He couldn't be certain how much whiskey he'd consumed, but no matter how much, it had to be one hundred percent more than he'd indulged in for a long time."

Once he cleaned up and shaved, he went into the sitting room just outside his bedroom door. He had to decide what to do next. Could he go back to Loveland as he'd vowed he would last night? Could he leave Virginia City without confronting Jesse with his feelings, without telling her nothing mattered but the love he felt for her?

To his surprise, a piece of paper lay on the floor. The note must have been slipped under the door sometime during the night. Cautiously, he picked it up, wondering if it could be from Jesse, saying she didn't want to see him again.

Russ—

Meet me in the dining room for breakfast. We need to talk about Laurel.

Jason

Russ shook his head. How Jesse must hate him. She even asked Jason to do the dirty work of telling him to leave. He'd been a fool, a real fool to think she still loved him. Somehow he knew last night, things would never be the same. Jesse wasn't the same. She'd become Laurel Morgan and from what he'd seen of the woman, he didn't like her.

Jesse, sweet loving Jesse, had become an elegant lady with no time for him or any man if he could believe Jason. They'd all hurt her more than she could ever forgive. It didn't matter he'd only been doing his duty when he arrested her father and brother and only carrying out the law when he watched them hang. They were her family, and he destroyed them. Why did he ever think she could begin to forgive him for such an act? She left him, changed her name, and ran away two years ago. What would stop her from doing the same thing again?

* * * *

By the light of day, The Mother Lode looked very different. People were sweeping up from the night before, getting ready for the night to come. Jason sat at a table in the dining room, and Russ knew he waited for him.

"Good morning, Russ," Jason said, getting to his feet and extending his hand. "What can we get you for breakfast?"

"I'm not hungry," Russ replied.

"Now look, if you're planning to see Laurel, you're going to eat," Jason declared, motioning to a waiter.

"Does she want to see me?" Russ said, defeat echoing in his voice. In his heart, he knew he'd given up hope of ever seeing Jesse again.

"Of course, she wants to see you. You're all she's talked about since she regained consciousness last night and again this morning when she woke up."

The waiter appeared at the table and Jason ordered two steak and egg breakfasts.

The act gave Russ time to think about what Jason just said. Russ knew Jason tried to read the expression on his face, but he purposely kept his eyes downcast until the waiter returned with two steaming mugs of coffee.

Jason waited until Russ took his first long drink before saying anything. "I gather you love her, and she loves you, so what are you going to do about it?"

"I'm not so certain you're right about Jesse still loving me. I'd thought of going back to Loveland today, not seeing her at all, letting sleeping dogs lie, so to say," Russ replied, his voice barely loud enough to be heard any further away than their table.

"You can't do such a thing to her. So now what?"

"I guess I'll confront her, try to start over, tell her how I feel." For the first time Russ looked into Jason's eyes. In them he could see a love for Jesse he thought only he could display.

"What if she doesn't want to go back to Loveland with you?" Jason said. "What if she wants to remain here even though she loves you?"

"There's nothing to keep me in Missouri. I think they'd just as soon have a new sheriff. I've spent the better part of the last two years running all over the country trying to find Jesse, following every lead. I know I love her, but what could I offer her if I came here? How can I come to her with nothing?"

"What if I could arrange something for you here?"

"Arrange something? Something like what? Being a bodyguard to someone like Laurel Morgan? No thank you. I'd rather find a job on one of the ranches doing something honest, something with my hands, rather than guarding some ice princess in an ivory tower."

"Do you really think Laurel is an ice princess in an ivory tower?"

"It certainly seems like it. You keep her locked up and guarded every minute. It looks as if you're afraid she'll run away."

"Perhaps it does, but the bodyguards aren't to keep Laurel a prisoner, they're to protect her from the men who think she's the most beautiful jewel they've ever seen. The men, who after a few drinks, think they'd like to spend some time with her, get to know her so to say."

Russ hung his head, shamed at his negative thoughts about Jason.

"I have no intention of offering you a position of bodyguard. There are good jobs available all around Virginia City. Do you want to be a country sheriff all your life?"

"No, but it's what I do best. I guess I could adjust to just about anything else, though."

"There's a Federal Marshal's office in town. It seems there's always an opening for a deputy. I figure the pay has be more than what Loveland, Missouri can afford to give its sheriff. I did some checking this morning, with a friend of mine there, and he says with your background, you could start any time you wanted."

"Do you always arrange other people's lives, Jason?" Russ said, smiling for the first time all morning.

"Only when they can't see for themselves what's best for them. You're miserable without Laurel, Laurel's miserable without you, and neither of you wants to make the first step. Someone has to intervene. So what do you say?"

"I say you have things all tied up in a pretty little package. If Jesse will have me, I'd have to do something and, if it means coming to Virginia City as the Federal Marshal, then that's what I'll do."

"You'd leave everything for Laurel?"

"I wouldn't leave everything for Laurel, I don't particularly like her. I'd leave everything for Jesse. In case you haven't noticed, they're two entirely different people."

Jason smiled. "I know all too well just how different they are. I suppose I can overlook Laurel's faults, because I created her. When I first met her, she carried herself well, but she wasn't the lady you saw last night. She was frightened and uncertain. It's taken two years for her to admit Jesse ever existed."

Breakfast came and, for a few minutes, they ate in silence, both thinking of the woman they loved.

"What happened last night?" Russ finally said.

"The doctor says it's exhaustion. Laurel feels it's because of what her brother did to her. It's another reason for her to stay here. Dr. Carrier is an excellent physician, and we're not too far from San Francisco or Salt Lake City. They have good doctors in both places. Maybe they can help her. Dr. Carrier even feels if she can come to grips with Jesse, it might help. She's so young, she deserves a good life."

"Do you think I'm too old for her?" Russ said.

Jason smiled, sadly. "I'm too old for her. For you, age doesn't matter when love is the main objective. If you love her, I'll do everything in my power to help you. If you don't love her, I'll personally make your life miserable if you ever hurt her."

They'd just finished eating and were getting better acquainted over a final cup of coffee, when a black woman entered the room.

"Miss Laurel wants to see you, Mr. Martin," she announced. "Sam will let you in, but don't you go upsettin' her."

"Russ, this is Sally Archer," Jason said, making the introductions. "She's Sam's wife and Laurel's personal maid, as well as her friend."

Russ stood and extended his hand to the woman. "No need to worry, Sally, I promise I'll be very gentle with her."

After excusing himself from the table, Russ hurried up the staircase. Standing outside Jesse's door, his stomach tried tying itself in knots the way it had three years ago in the little church in Clarkston. He wanted to see her, to hold her, to tell her nothing had changed, and yet he had to know the truth first. He had to know why she'd left Loveland. Why she deserted him? Why she gave up on God?

Hesitantly, he knocked on her door. He expected to hear her say, 'come in,' but instead, the door opened. Standing in front of him, he saw Jesse. Jesse as he remembered her, as he'd dreamed of her. Not Laurel Morgan, but Jesse, her face scrubbed and her hair hanging loose around her shoulders.

"Jesse," he said, as he studied her face.

Her brilliant smile faded. She saw him and tears brimmed in her green eyes. She put her hand, tentatively, to the stitches in his cheek.

"Russ," she whispered. "Oh, Russ, I've hurt you so badly." With those words, she started to turn away. Gently, he turned her back toward him and held her while she cried.

"Are you so afraid of me, Jesse? Why is it when you see me you cry and shake like a leaf?"

Her silver cane clattered to the floor, as her arms went around his neck, allowing him to support her weight. "Afraid of you? Oh, Russ, I love you too much to ever be afraid."

"You sure have a strange way of showing it," he said, as he swept her into his arms and carried her into the bedroom. Even in his arms, she continued to cry and to shake. Carefully, he laid her on the freshly made bed, propping her up with pillows. Sitting beside her, he picked up a lace handkerchief from the bedside table and gently wiped her eyes.

"There's no reason to cry, Jesse."

"Yes, there is. Jason told me what happened at The Gilded Lily last night. He told me how Jake hurt you. I'm so sorry, so very sorry."

"What do you mean Jason told you? You were there. You saw what happened."

"I remember nothing of what went on there last night, Russ. Nothing after I left The Mother Lode, except for the coldness, the stars, and praying you would forgive me."

Russ couldn't help laughing at the irony of the situation. "I didn't know. I came to ask you to forgive me for what I said last night and you don't even remember it."

"My words weren't kind either," Jesse said. "I don't want to know what you said. I want this to be the first time I've seen you, the first time you've seen me. Things were easier when you breezed into my life the way you did in Clarkston. I had no time to think."

Russ thought for a minute. Knowing Clarkston still held a special memory for Jesse as it did for him, brought him pleasure.

"Three years ago, on Easter Sunday, I heard an angel sing and I decided to marry her. Then I saw her talking to a younger man and wondered what I could ever offer her. I experienced those same feelings last night when I heard you sing, when I realized what you've become and saw how many people love you."

Russ paused for a minute before he asked the questions which were on his mind. "Why did you leave, Jesse? Why did you make it so hard for me to find you?"

Jesse closed her eyes, as though the answer to Russ' questions would hurt him and she needed time to decide how to phrase her answer.

"I doubt if you'll believe me. I could never fault you for your disbelief. I left because I love you."

"You're right, your reason is hard to believe. Can you explain it?"

"I know you've bent the law more than once for me. You've made allowances you didn't have to make. You did things, which weren't exactly proper, and for those things I love you. I love you so much I'd planned to leave Clarkston and go on to Denver, never staying in Loveland, but you know all about those plans, you helped me change them. What you don't know is why."

Russ continued to hold her hand, trying to remain calm, not to push her too hard. "Are you going to tell me why?"

She nodded, then continued. "I had planned to go to Denver, because I couldn't stand being in the same town with you and not be able to love you."

Jesse paused giving Russ a chance to interrupt. "I still don't understand. You were able to love me, at least I thought you loved me, and yet you asked me to wait. When you finally said you would marry me, you disappeared. How can you call your actions love?"

"You must remember it all happened three years ago. I didn't know who Jesse Tyler was, other than a frightened child. I had no idea what being a wife or even a woman entailed. I didn't even know what it meant to love someone. I couldn't love you then, not the way you deserved to be loved."

Jesse cried at what must have been a bitter memory for her, but Russ made no attempt to comfort her. Her words saddened and hurt him too much for that kind of reaction.

"And a year later, when you left, how did you feel then?"

"On the morning Caleb and Frank arrived, I'd been so happy. We were making plans to be married, and for the first time I knew what love meant. They changed everything. How could I say I love you, Russ, I still want to marry you, when I'd become what I so despised? I saw the look in your eyes when you pulled my gun from Ruben's belt. I'd hurt you, disobeyed you. I, more than anyone, knew what disobedience meant. I'd just taken a beating at Frank's hands for disobeying, for shooting Caleb. I knew I could never live with any unspoken accusations between us. I knew you could never live with anyone who was capable of murder."

Russ had tears in his eyes, but he made no attempt to wipe them before he pulled her into his arms and kissed away her fears. "When I saw Ruben had your gun, I experienced a sense of relief. I'd been so afraid you weren't able to protect yourself from them. I never thought you misunderstood my relief for repulsion. When I first heard the shots, not one, but two, I thought you were dead. When I saw you with Frank, I knew he'd hurt you, but you were alive, and I had to find a way to keep you alive. You hurt me most when you didn't want to see me, when you disappeared, when I found your Bible."

Jesse interrupted. "You still don't understand. Maybe you never will, but to me it made perfect sense. Frank took everything from me, my self-respect, and my faith—"

Russ silenced her with a tender kiss. Maybe he'd never understand, as she said, but right now, he wanted no more explanations. He wanted to comfort her, to love her, to hold her.

"Let me finish, Russ, hear the whole story before you make any decisions," she begged as she pulled away from him.

He held her at arms' length, and studied her face, noting the haunted expression in her eyes. "Are you going to tell me about the lies you told Madam DuPre?"

"How did you know about her?"

"Did you think I wouldn't look for you? I found her after you left. She told me about Kate Cross. She thought I was the husband who'd beaten you so severely. She sent me to New Orleans, but then I lost you. I've chased every red haired woman within five hundred miles of Loveland. I've met a schoolteacher in Garden City, a nanny in New Orleans, a woman in Pecos, and a dozen more I don't even remember. When Quaid said he'd found you, everyone, even Gary, was skeptical, but I knew it had to be you. I prayed it would be you. I had to have you tell me, face to face, you didn't want me."

"Oh, Russ, I never stopped loving you," she said, choking on her tears. "It took two years, but I'm finally coming to grips with Jesse. I'd decided to contact you and beg your forgiveness. After last night's show, before Jason came to tell me you were here, I even started to write you a letter, but putting my feelings on paper seemed too hard to do."

"Are you ready to come back to Loveland?"

"I may never be ready to return to Loveland. There are too many bad memories and ghosts associated with that place. Even with Gary waiting for me, I know I couldn't go back. I also know I can't ask you to give up your life for me."

Russ again held her close. The truth hurt, but at the same time, it healed. He'd been afraid of what she had to tell him, afraid she would lie to spare his feelings. Laurel Morgan had been a lie, but the words she just spoke belonged to Jesse, and he knew them to be true.

"I already knew what you'd say. I only wanted to hear you say the words," he said, reassuringly.

"How could you know?"

"Jason told me."

"Jason talks too much," she said, suppressing a nervous laugh.

"You said you couldn't ask me to give up my life for you, but if this trip had turned out like all the others, I would have left Loveland and started over someplace else. If after two years, I hadn't found you, I knew I never would. Marry me, Jesse. Marry me today. We can go back to Loveland and close our lives there, then come back here and start fresh."

For the first time, Jesse laughed out loud. Her laughter sounded good to him. "Are you telling me you'd be content to be married to Laurel Morgan?"

Russ put his hand on her cheek. "No, but I'd like to get to know her better. I want to be married to you, Jesse. I want to care for and protect you. If a little of Laurel Morgan brushed off on you, so be it. Jason thinks it's best if you stay in Virginia City. He loves you. I can tell it in his voice. He also knows Jesse and Laurel will someday be one. Once you realize the same thing, Laurel will, more than likely, become little more than a pleasant memory."

"How can I say no to you, Russ? How can I deny my feelings any longer?"

"Give me an hour to find a minister..."

Jesse tensed in his arms. "A justice of the peace," she corrected him.

"No, Jesse, a minister. The Jesse Tyler I know would insist on one."

"The Jesse you knew hadn't sinned so grossly, hadn't done things no one, not even God could forgive."

Russ shook his head. "Dear, dear Jesse, a few minutes ago, you said you prayed for forgiveness. Give God a chance. Let Him reenter your life. It seems to me you need what I have in my room. You should get reacquainted with your mother's Bible, while Jason and I plan the wedding."

* * * *

Although Russ insisted Jesse take the worn Bible, she could not find the courage to open it. She wanted God's forgiveness, but asking for it seemed an impossible obstacle to overcome.

Everything happened so quickly, Jesse had trouble keeping all of it straight. Jason helped Russ secure a position with the Federal Marshal's office and then presented them with a grand house.

"I built it when I first came to Virginia City," he explained. "I thought someday I would settle down, remarry, and bring a wife here. It never happened. I fell in love with The Mother Lode. Take the house and fill it with love. Let it be my wedding present to you."

The wedding had been a small, private affair. Sally stood as Jesse's matron of honor and cried when Jesse gave herself to the man she loved. It was Quaid who acted as Russ' best man. Jason gave the bride away and the wedding guests were the employees of The Mother Lode.

The only thing marring their happiness were the rumors about Jesse, which were circulating around Virginia City. There had been only one performance on Saturday evening, followed by the scene at The Gilded Lily. The two events had everyone in town talking. Mainly people wanted to know Laurel Morgan's true identity.

To put the rumors to rest, once and for all, Jesse insisted they arrange a special performance for Thursday evening. The dining room easily filled to capacity with invited guests. People who'd been loyal patrons and admirers for the last two years, now waited with baited breath to hear the true story behind their favorite songbird.

For the first time, Jesse dined with the guests, sitting at a table with Russ, Jason, and Quaid. When people, whom she'd only seen from the stage stopped to talk, she beamed.

With dinner ended, Jason and Russ assisted her in mounting the steps to take her usual place on stage.

"Welcome to The Mother Lode," Jason began. "Tonight you are my guests. I'm certain you've all heard the rumors. The time has come, when Laurel wants you to know the truth."

As Jesse began to tell her story, women cried, and at times, Jesse stopped her narrative to wipe her eyes.

"Russ Martin and I were married yesterday and we're going back to Missouri to close our lives there. When we return, I'm afraid Laurel Morgan will not be singing on this stage. I'm trying desperately to find Jesse Tyler. To find her, I must put Laurel Morgan in her proper place.

You've all been very loyal to me, but I must ask you to wish me well and welcome me back as a member of this community."

The applause seemed deafening, the cheers encouraging. To Jesse's surprise, the entire audience was on their feet, applauding.

"Sing one last song, Laurel," someone called.

Russ hadn't left her side. He'd stood by her, supporting her, while she said the words, which hurt so badly. "I'd like to hear Laurel sing, too," he whispered in her ear.

Chapter Twenty-one

Jesse rested her head against Russ' arm. The trip had been exhausting, reliving the past trying. Moments earlier the conductor announced they would be arriving in Loveland. Now she wondered what lay ahead of her.

When the train stopped, they made their way down the crowded aisle and stepped into the bright sunlight of the Missouri afternoon. Anxiously, she looked around to find Gary. As soon as she caught his eye, she called his name.

He hurried to her side and hugged her tightly. "Oh Jes, you're home. Home for good."

"No, Gary. I'm not home for good. Loveland is no longer my home."

"Then what's going on? You're with Russ. Didn't the two of you get married?"

"We'll explain everything when we get out to the farm," Russ said, shaking Gary's hand. "Just help me with this baggage, and we'll be ready to go."

"The farm? We're not going out to the farm. Clara and the children are at your place. She wanted to tidy things up before Jesse got home."

Jesse could feel her excitement over seeing Gary turn to despair at the thought of going back to the shop.

"Jesse isn't ready to go there yet," Russ said.

"It will be all right, Russ. I have to face it sometime." Jesse declared, hoping her voice sounded more confident than she felt. She turned back to Gary. "Russ told me about Laura. Has Clara had the baby?"

Gary nodded. "Three weeks ago. We named him Eli. He reminds me of you. He has fiery red hair and a mind of his own."

* * * *

Once they arrived at the house and sat down to eat, Jesse seemed uneasy. Under the table, Russ grasped her hand, trying to reassure her. He wondered if she would be strong enough to enter the shop, or if he should insist they go to the farm as soon as they finished eating.

"Now, what's going on?" Gary demanded, once grace had been said and their plates filled.

Russ looked at Jesse before he began. "In Virginia City, I met a girl by the name of Laurel Morgan."

"Do you know this Laurel Morgan, Jes?" concern sounded in Gary's voice.

"I know her very well," Jesse replied, a bit of mischief in her eyes.

Russ again squeezed her hand and then continued. "I fell in love with her and we were married."

Gary's face fell. "Are you married, Jes?"

"Yes," she giggled. "I'm sorry, Gary, we shouldn't tease you. I'm Laurel Morgan."

Russ watched Gary's face. He didn't look particularly amused at their private joke. He appeared annoyed with them.

"We didn't expect you to understand," Russ said. "We brought along this article from the Virginia City newspaper."

Gary reached across the table and took the clipping from Russ' hand, as soon as he removed it from the pocket of his vest.

"Read it aloud, Gary," Clara prompted.

Gary scanned the article, then his voice filled with disbelief. "Virginia City's own Miss Laurel Morgan, turns out to be the daughter of Caleb Tyler, the outlaw, who was hanged two years ago in Loveland, Missouri. The lovely songbird who ran away from her past, arrived in Virginia City shortly thereafter and has enchanted her audiences ever since.

"Last evening, to an audience of local patrons, she announced her marriage to a Russell Martin, of Loveland, Missouri. After a prolonged wedding trip, she will be returning to Virginia City, but she has said good-bye to The Mother Lode. We wish you luck and happiness, Laurel."

Gary put the clipping down on the table, his face white, and his eyes angry. "I don't know what to say to you, Jes."

Jesse's smile seemed dazzling. Russ recognized it as what he called her Laurel Morgan smile. "Tell us you're happy for us."

"You're planning to go back to Virginia City, aren't you?" Gary said, as though he hadn't heard her words.

"I have a life there, Gary," she replied, her smile fading. "I don't like being apart from you, but there are some very bad memories here. You have everything you want in Loveland, but I—"

"I thought you did, too, Jes," Gary interrupted, cutting her short. "You have the shop, Russ, what more could you want?"

"The dress shop is an impossible dream. Frank made it impossible. I'll never be able to sew again. As for Russ, I haven't lost him."

It still seemed as though Gary couldn't comprehend the situation. "Are you going back to Virginia City as well, Russ?"

"I have a job as a deputy United States Marshal waiting for me when we get back. I had no trouble getting the position with my background and a little help from Jesse's friend." He wished Gary would take the time to see what they were doing would be for the best.

"Your friend, Jes?"

"The man who befriended me. Jason Bellinger has been very kind to me. He kept my secret for two years, even though I thought he didn't know. He runs The Mother Lode, the place where I worked."

"The Mother Lode? It sounds like a dance hall. Are you a dance hall girl? Is that what gives you satisfaction. Do you enjoy being pawed by dozens of men at night?" Without waiting for an answer, Gary threw his napkin on the table and stormed out of the kitchen.

Russ and Jesse both stood to follow him. "Stay here, Honey," Russ said. "Let me talk to him."

"Now listen to me, Gary," Russ said, once he followed Gary into the shop. "The Mother Lode is an elegant gaming club and restaurant. No one, but no one would dare paw Miss Laurel." He touched his cheek and ran his hand over the place where Jake hit him. "I should know, I have the scars to prove it."

Neither of them saw Jesse follow them and were unaware of her presence until she put her hand on Gary's arm. "You must understand my life in Virginia City was very different from any I've ever lived before. I had around the clock bodyguards so no one could get near me."

"A singer couldn't possible have been worth enough to warrant such an expense. What other favors were you expected to give this Jason Bellinger?" Gary spat, making her life sound tainted and dirty.

"I dealt Black Jack five nights a week until Jason told me he thought it too much for me. Once I started singing two shows on Saturday nights, I only dealt cards three nights."

Gary looked astonished. "How could you do such a thing? I may be pretty new at being a Christian, but I do know good girls don't play black jack or sing in taverns. Don't you understand God doesn't approve of people like you?"

"For the last two years I lost sight of God. It wasn't until I thought I might lose Russ that I turned to Him again. The article said I wouldn't be returning to The Mother Lode. The reason is I couldn't be faithful to God and work in a gaming club, too. How can I make you understand my life?"

Russ looked into Jesse's eyes, worried about the confrontation. Would she ever be ready to face her past? They'd planned to see the shop together, with no one else around. They agreed to wait until she considered herself ready. Now they were here, here with Gary and Clara, here before he thought she should be.

"You'll never understand, Gary, because you don't want to understand," she shouted, her composure beginning to drain, her words beginning to slur. "They came in here and took everything I'd worked so hard to achieve. They took my self-respect in less time than it takes for me to do a show. Caleb and Frank killed Jesse Tyler. You weren't here. You didn't see the look in Caleb's eyes, or hear the hatred in Frank's voice. How can I ever hope to explain what it was like to relive it every day since it happened. Being here with the memories would be sheer torture, being in Virginia City with them, makes them almost bearable."

Jesse crossed the room, touching the things she left behind. Gary started to go to her, but Russ stopped him. He knew the process had begun, now she needed to finish what she'd started. Absently, she opened the drawer of the sewing table, and Russ remembered the pearl handled gun he'd left there.

Jesse caressed the handle of the gun. Before her, flashed the scenes she'd relived so many times since the shooting. She could hear Caleb calling her 'Jesse Girl', coming closer and closer until she pulled the gun from the drawer. She could hear herself telling him to stay away, feel her finger tightening on the trigger until the sound of the explosion echoed in her ears. In her mind, not only could she hear the explosion, but she could feel the kick of the gun in her hand, see the blood that splattered both her and the shop, and feel the pain of Frank's vice-like grip. As the memories flooded over her, she began to cry, uncontrollably.

"It doesn't go away. Why doesn't it ever go away?" she cried, choking on her own tears.

Russ hurried to her side, concerned over what he just witnessed. Taking her in his arms he whispered words of encouragement in her ear. As he expected, she became limp as conscious thought left her body. Sweeping her into his arms, he carried her out of the room, past a bewildered Gary.

Carefully, he laid her on the bed. As he did, her eyes fluttered open. "Everything will be all right," he assured her, gently stroking her hair.

In his heart, he knew it would never be all right. He should have never let her go to the shop. He should have insisted they go directly to Gary's farm. He should have told Gary the truth about Jesse. He knew all the things he should have done, but didn't do. It was good to see Jesse having fun with her little game of pretense. Letting Gary wonder if they'd actually gotten married. That, he thought, had been Laurel Morgan's doing. Laurel's self-centered idea of fun. Laurel's knack for getting her own way.

"Russ," she whispered. "It was horrible."

"It's over now, Jesse. You won't ever have to face it again I'd forgotten about the gun. I'm sorry."

"The gun?" Jesse said, as if she didn't remember. "The gun, yes it was hard to see it, to touch it. It wasn't as hard as being in that room, though. It seemed so terrible, so hard to accept."

Russ continued to talk quietly to her. When Clara entered the room, he took the glass she brought him.

Mixing a packet of sleeping powder into the water, he continued. "You're going to sleep now, Jesse."

"Are you going to make me take the medicine?" she said.

"Dr. Carrier made me promise. It will get better." He held the glass to her lips, and waited until she finished all of the contents.

Once it was empty, he set the glass on the table beside the bed and held her hand as she relaxed. Dr. Carrier had prepared him. He told him the medicine would take effect quickly, considering her exhaustion.

When at last she fell asleep, he laid her hand on the bed and covered her with a light quilt from the closet.

He left the room, closing the door behind him. Upon entering the parlor, he saw Gary and Dr. Page coming into the house through the back door.

"Hello, Doc," Russ said. Even to him, his voice sounded weary.

"Russ," Dr. Page replied, shaking his hand. "Gary says I have a patient here."

"Not really, she's fallen asleep. When she wakes up, she'll be fine."

"FINE?" Gary echoed. "How can you stand there and tell me she'll be fine? I saw her in there."

"You've seen only a fraction of what I have since I found her. She isn't well. I think it's time I told you about Jesse Tyler, Laurel Morgan, Kate Cross, and any other names she might have used."

Gary sat down at the table, his hand trembling, and his face ashen. Clara had cleared away the dishes and put the children down in the parlor for their naps before she joined them, bringing steaming mugs of coffee.

"Caleb and Frank hurt her badly. Not just physically, but mentally as well. As a child, her fear had been having Caleb take her away. When the fear became reality, she began to build a fragile shell around herself. I doubt any of us ever knew the real Jesse Tyler. She thought she had nowhere to turn. You were there to take the brunt of it, but it scared her.

"When she left, I think she would have welcomed a hangman's noose. Anything would have been better than what she'd already endured. Then, suddenly, I told her she had no guilt. It was just a fact. She didn't prove herself innocent, the way you did. I told her she hadn't been wanted, she wouldn't hang. It proved to be only the first blow she took. I think it had to be the reason she didn't want to return from Clarkston. Maybe it would have been better if she went to Denver and disappeared. Of course, they say all things happen for a reason.

"When she came back here, she began to feel secure. We let her know she was loved, accepted, and it seemed to be all she ever wanted. Just when we were making progress, Caleb and Frank returned to her life. It looked like everything she worked so hard to achieve would be taken away.

"Leaving here and changing her name all seemed rational at the time. She needed to run away, not from you or me, but from herself. She can consider herself lucky God sent kind people to help her along the way.

"Madam DuPre pitied Kate Cross, and you can't blame her. We know the condition she was in when she left. The cuts, the bruises, the broken wrist, all made her story about an abusive husband believable.

"As for Jason Bellinger, he knew her identity, and he knew her reasons for running away. Rather than turn her in, he helped her. He took her to Virginia City and gave her something she'd never had before, self-respect. She wasn't a tavern girl. She certainly wasn't a girl in one of the upstairs rooms. She became Laurel Morgan, an elegant lady, loved by everyone. Jason created her, because he loved her. He loves her, as does everyone who knows her. God sent him, as well as people like Sally, her maid, Sam, Jake, and Slim her bodyguards, and all the people who came to hear her sing, to love and protect her.

"Jason kept her secret, even from her, for two years. He never tried to bridge the past until the day I arrived. Why he did then, we'll never know. He says he thought she'd become ready to face her past. Maybe he had the right idea.

"I didn't care for Laurel when I first met her. Doubt you would have liked her either. She appeared to be selfish, beautiful, and pampered. I wanted Jesse back, and I thought I'd never have her. I feared Laurel had destroyed her. Little by little, the protective shell began to crack and peel away so Jesse could reappear."

Gary shook his head, as if trying to picture Jesse as Laurel. "What about this spell she had today?"

"It's part of facing Jesse. The first time it happened, I didn't see it.

I'd been a fool. I'd downed half a bottle of whiskey in the time it took her to walk down the street to find me. I wanted to tell her the truth. Only I went about it the wrong way. I grabbed her arm and swore I'd make her tell me what I wanted to hear. I hadn't planned on what she meant to the people of Virginia City. Even in a rowdy tavern like The Gilded Lily, she'd been protected. Before I could get her to the door, the bartender had a shotgun pointed at me. He told me I wasn't taking her anywhere. When I turned toward the door, this big ox, by the name of Jake, came in. By the time I came to, she'd disappeared. I thought I'd lost her forever. Of course, Jason had taken her back to The Mother Lode because she'd collapsed, like she did today.

"Once she regained consciousness, she admitted every time she became tired or thought about Jesse, she got dizzy. Her confession became the beginning of the break through for us. Little by little she's been facing up to her past.

"After we were married and left Virginia City, we didn't come straight here. We went to Stillwater first. There she found Ed's grave and I said good-bye to Ellie. I thought Dr. Carrier had been mistaken. I thought the worst of it was over, since she seemed unshaken. I hadn't stopped to realize she barely knew Ed.

"Slack Creek was a different story. What I saw there wasn't as bad as what you saw here, but it seemed like it at the time. Finding Clay and Will, realizing it had been Clay who planted the seed of Jesse Tyler in my mind to give her a chance at a decent life, hit her hard. It took almost two days before we could leave the hotel and come here.

"I can only thank God, she doesn't remember her feelings when she first confronts her past. When she wakes up, although she'll have no memory of what happened, she'll be able to accept who she is.

"We knew the shop would be difficult. I'd forgotten about the gun, though. I could see it in her eyes, she relived every minute of the day she shot Caleb. Luckily, she'll sleep now."

"How can you be so certain she'll sleep, Russ?" Dr. Page inquired.

"Dr. Carrier gave us these," Russ replied, handing him the empty packet.

Dr. Page examined it carefully. "This is a very strong sedative. Are you positive Jesse can handle it?"

"It allows her the rest she needs. It helps her to relax. Before we leave, she has a lot to face up to. Friends, family, even Caleb and Frank. Once we finish here, we can go home."

"Home?" Clara questioned. "If she accepts her past, why can't you stay here?"

"Because she's very happy in Virginia City. She's facing up to her past, but it will take a long time for the healing to be complete. Dr. Carrier feels coming to grips with it will be the beginning."

"What do you think, Russ?" Dr. Page said.

"I tend to agree with him. She's better now than before. None of us can be certain. No one knows much about the mind."

* * * *

Jesse woke slowly. To her surprise, she recalled everything vividly. She was in Loveland, in the little house at the end of Main Street. She remembered going to the shop as well as her tears, Russ' concern, and the sleeping powder. The memory made her smile, knowing she'd never been able to remember any of what occurred when she encountered the past. Dr. Carrier had been right, facing the past did have a healing effect.

On the dresser a lamp burned, illuminating the room, warding off the shadows of the early evening. The mantel clock began to strike and she counted eight chimes. The day was over, she'd slept it away. Instead of the feeling of desperation, she usually felt after such a sleep, she was, for the first time, rested.

Taking the lamp, she left the bedroom and entered the parlor. She heard voices coming from the porch. In the fading light, see the glow of Gary's cigarette and smelled Russ' pipe. Although she couldn't make out the words, she didn't care. She only hoped they weren't talking about her, or concerned for her. She realized Clara and the children must have gone back to the farm. At least she hoped they had because it was surely time for them to be in their beds.

To Jesse's left stood the closed door that led to the shop. Tentatively she opened it and entered. She held the lamp high, so its light could illuminate the room and chase the shadows from the corners.

* * * *

Gary finished his cigarette and flipped it harmlessly to the dirt beside the porch. Russ watched as the red glow of the cigarette burned itself out in the dirt he had been certain Jesse would fill with flowers when she moved back into the house. Seeing it now, with the knowledge they would soon be leaving, made him realize it would remain barren for yet another year.

"We should go back in and check on Jesse," he said, tapping his pipe against the railing. "She should be waking up any time now."

"What will happen then?" Gary said.

"Like I told you, she'll remember nothing. I explained about Slack Creek. I didn't tell you what happened when we were finally able to leave the hotel. We went back to the cemetery—"

"You took her back?"

"It's part of the process. Once she faced it, even though she couldn't remember it, she could accept it. It will be the same here. She'll shake, she'll cry, and she'll accept it. Dr. Carrier didn't know if it would work, but it has. It's exactly what happened the first time, when she confronted me. It's strange what the mind can do. We can only guess at what to do for her and pray it works."

"How can you be so certain she won't remember any of it?" Gary demanded.

Russ could tell from his expression, he couldn't comprehend anyone blanking out such an emotional scene, especially Jesse. "It's happened before. I wish she would remember, so does Dr. Carrier. When we get back, if he doesn't feel this trip has helped, Jason is ready to send for a specialist from San Francisco."

"Jesse's always been the strong one. I envied her strength. I thought it came from her faith, her trust in God."

"Some of it did. Mostly, it was an act. When Caleb and Frank confronted her the last time, they put her over the edge. They made her question herself, her faith, everything. I knew coming here would be the worst part of the trip for her. I also knew it was something she had to do."

Together, they entered the house and were surprised to see a light coming from the shop. Hurrying to the door, they watched Jesse walking around the room, touching everything, as if for the first time.

"Jesse," Russ said softly.

When she turned, Russ noticed the look of surprise on Gary's face to see the Jesse he remembered. Her radiance, her smile, even the sparkle in her eyes said Jesse had finally returned to them.

"Are you all right, Honey?" Russ took her in his arms.

"I can't believe it, Russ. I remember everything that happened, absolutely everything." Jesse seemed to laughing and crying at the same time.

"I don't know what to say," Russ said.

"It's just a room, Russ, a room with tables and chairs and a dressmaker's dummy. There is nothing to fear here. Even the ghosts are gone. The nightmares may not be over, but I can be in this room. Do you think this means I'm healing?"

"Yes," Russ assured her. "I definitely think this means you're healing."

* * * *

"You gave us quite a scare," Gary said, hugging her tightly.

"Remembering has been frightening for me as well. Has it been this bad before?"

Russ nodded. "It hasn't been easy, but your remembering is worth everything."

"Now can we persuade you to stay here, Jes?" Gary said.

"I don't think so, Gary. My life is in Virginia City. I owe Jason far too much not to return there."

"Dr. Page came while you were asleep," Gary continued, disappointment in her statement evident in his voice. "He wants to see you."

"I plan to see him tomorrow," she replied.

"No fuss?" Gary exclaimed. "Is this my sister talking? The last time I mentioned seeing Dr. Page, my life didn't seem to be worth very much."

"A lot has happened. I've learned sometimes doctors are necessary."

"Just how did you learn it, Jes? Did Laurel Morgan teach you, or did you learn it from your friend Jason, what's-his-name?"

Jesse understood Gary's confusion. She hadn't expected him to accept Laurel, but she needed to help him understand her. Sitting at the table, she held his hand and began to explain, while Russ prepared a plate of food for her.

"I'm certain Russ told you all about Laurel Morgan, and I'm just as certain you don't understand. I went to a strange town and changed my name, my life. I became the person I pretended to be. Even though I became what everyone wanted me to be, inside, I remained Jesse Tyler. When I go back to Virginia City, Jesse and Laurel will finally be one.

"When I lived as Laurel, I hid Jesse. I thought if I didn't have any of her traits, no one would ever know she existed. No one would guess how ugly her past had been. I only fooled myself. I know that now. I can't hide from the past. It happened and I'm facing up to it. It isn't easy. I rode with Caleb, I did almost everything he told me to do, and I shot him. Those things don't make me a bad person, only a frightened child, who did what her father told her to do. I can understand it and accept it."

They talked on for a long time, until at last, Gary left for home. It had been a long day, an eventful day. Even though Jesse slept the afternoon away, she knew sleep would come readily once she was in bed. After she and Russ made long delightful love, she fell asleep in the comfort of his arms.

Chapter Twenty-two

"Good morning, beautiful," Russ greeted Jesse, when he brought her a breakfast tray. "How do you feel?"

"Happy, very happy. What did you do with the colt, Russ? I found it in the drawer before you gave me the medication, but when I woke up it was gone."

Russ held her hand, pressing it to his lips for a long moment before he answered. "I sent it home with Gary. I didn't think I should keep it here. I couldn't be certain how you'd feel about it."

"You know Gary shouldn't have a gun. You seem to be bending the law again. What kind of a lawman are you?"

Russ laughed at her question. "A cautious one. Gary knows the provisions of his freedom and so do I. He has the gun put safely away, until such time as I think you should have it. Now, eat your breakfast. We have a busy day ahead of us."

At noon, they met Gary at the cafe. When they finished eating, Jesse insisted they take her to the cemetery. Both Russ and Gary expressed their doubts about her going there. Once she stood in front of the markers, she remained dry eyed.

She read aloud the words written on them. Each read the same with the exception of the dates of birth and the names. HANGED FOR MURDER - APRIL 16, 1888.

"There were rewards for them, you know," Russ said, later in the evening, when they were alone. "Gary got half and half is for you. It comes to close to a thousand dollars."

"I don't want it. I don't want any part of it. Does my decision upset you?"

"You know it doesn't. I thought you might feel this way. Don't make any decision right now. The money won't be going anywhere."

"I have more money than I will ever need. I used very little of the salary Jason paid me. There was no need. Whatever I wanted, Jason provided. It's all sitting in the bank in Virginia City. With all of that, why should I want Caleb's blood money?"

"You earned it."

"Earned it? Hardly. I shot Caleb before he could take me back to Mexico. I certainly don't call that earning it. I can't take it, but I can put it in Laura and Eli's names. We'll call it a legacy from their Grandmother Tyler."

Russ laughed out loud. "I guess that's why I love you, Jesse. You aren't nearly as selfish as Laurel pretends to be."

Jesse wandered back into the shop. "I can hardly believe I ever called this house my home," she said, again touching the items. "It's strange, it seems as though someone else lived here, someone else shot Caleb, and yet I know there was no one else, only me."

"At the time, I think you were someone else, Jesse. Maybe it's a good thing you went away and became Laurel for a time. The Jesse who lived in this house has grown into a beautiful woman. One I'm proud to call my wife."

Jesse closed her eyes and allowed Russ to take her into his arms. For the first time in years a feeling of total peace came over her.

You were only away for a little while, a voice within her mind sounded. *Like Russ, you had to experience the pain, before you could return to my loving arms. Although it seemed as though I left you, I was never far from your side. During the bad times, I protected you and sent people like Madam Dupre and Jason to keep you safe from harm.*

"It's over," Jesse whispered. "I know God loves me and He was never far from my side. For a while I was too blind to see how He loved and protected me."

Russ held her at arm's length. "Are you certain?"

Jesse nodded.

"Knowing you lost your faith, when you did so much to help me to again find mine, was the hardest part of losing you. I knew how important God had always been to you. He brought you through the

166

years of riding with Caleb. I could never understand how you could so easily forsake Him after—"

"After I shot Caleb?" Jesse said, finishing Russ' statement with a question. "Caleb and Frank reminded me of how grossly I had sinned. In a few moments I broke three of the Commandments, three of the rules I lived by all my life. 'Honor thy father and thy mother.' Caleb reminded me he was my father, even if I didn't want to admit it. Frank reminded me, 'Thou shalt not kill' and 'Thou shalt not bear false witness'. In a matter of a few minutes, I not only denounced my father, but I shot him. I told some terrible lies. I didn't know if I had killed him, but it didn't matter. At the time, I wanted to kill him. I didn't think God could ever forgive anyone who had done those things. I remembered telling Clay he would go to Hell for the things he'd done. How could I expect any different treatment?"

"And now? How do you feel now?"

"From within, I heard a voice which told me He had never left me, would never leave me. I'm safe. Between you and God, I won't ever be afraid again."

About the Author

Mild Mannered wife, mother, and grandmother by day, Sherry Derr-Wille spends her nights writing and writing and writing. Having been inspired by an English assignment in her sophomore year of high school, she had never quite finished the assignment. New stories pop into her head every day with never enough time to write them all.

A Wisconsin native, she grew up a country girl, but enjoys her "city" home. She and her husband of almost 50 years, Bob, live in a mid-sized town close to the Illinois border, where she works as a receptionist for an insurance office and he is retired. Deeming Bob "A Saint" for putting up with her she has never regretted marrying her high school sweetheart just two days after graduation in 1964.

www.derr-wille.com

Read more by this author at
www.melange-books.com

Hattie's Preacher, The Outlaw Series, Book 1
Outlaw's Son, The Outlaw Series, Book 2

www.ingramcontent.com/pod-product-compliance
Lightning Source LLC
Chambersburg PA
CBHW032204190626
46810CB00018B/1464